*A
Harlequin
Romance*

OTHER
Harlequin Romances

by LUCY GILLEN

Many of these titles are available at your local bookseller,
or through the Harlequin Reader Service.

For a free catalogue listing all available Harlequin Romances,
send your name and address to:

HARLEQUIN READER SERVICE,
M.P.O. Box 707, Niagara Falls, N.Y. 14302
Canadian address: Stratford, Ontario, Canada N5A 6W4

or use order coupon at back of books.

RETURN TO DEEPWATER

by

LUCY GILLEN

Harlequin Books

TORONTO • LONDON • NEW YORK • AMSTERDAM • SYDNEY • WINNIPEG

Original hardcover edition published in 1975
by Mills & Boon Limited

ISBN 0-373-02012-0

Harlequin edition published October 1976

CHAPTER ONE

TARIN was aware that her uncle was watching her and had been ever since they sat down to their meal. She had been gazing out of the window at the vastness of the open moorland where it swept right down as far as the ragged hedge that surrounded her uncle's garden. The sight of it was all very familiar and yet somehow different from how she remembered it, and she supposed the contradiction in terms was due to her own maturing. The last time she had seen it through the eyes of a child, now she was a grown woman and it had a different aspect.

She turned her head suddenly and smiled at her uncle seated on the other side of the table, and thought that the same curious contradiction applied to him too. Robert McCourt was her father's youngest brother and so very much like him that it had startled her several times since her arrival, because she did not remember him being so much like him before.

Tall and good-looking, he had the McCourt head of thick, dark brown hair that Tarin herself had inherited, only his eyes were brown like her father's, while Tarin had inherited her own deep blue ones from her mother.

She had spent so many happy holidays up here in Scotland, in the little village of Deepwater, with her uncle and Aunt Margaret. After Aunt Margaret died her uncle had become something of a recluse for quite a long time, but in the last year he had once more started to correspond with his brothers and their families. It had been Uncle Robert who mentioned that there was an advert in the local newspaper for a secretary, and jokingly wondered who would want to bury themselves in the wilds of the Scottish Highlands to work for Darrel Bruce.

Not that Robert McCourt really considered living in Scotland as being buried at all, for he had always resolutely refused to leave his native heath for more prosperous fields, and unlike his brothers, including Tarin's father, he had never felt the need to seek pastures new. He was content and happy in his own environment.

In writing about the advertised job, however, he had reckoned without his niece's impulsiveness, and knew nothing of her memories. No one could have been more surprised when he learned from his brother that Tarin had actually applied for the post he had so casually mentioned, but he had lost no time in assuring her that she would be more than welcome to stay with him for as long as she cared to. Certainly until she had been to the house for an interview with Darrel Bruce.

No one actually living in the village ever referred to Deepwater as anything else but 'the house', and even in the short time she had been back Tarin found herself falling in with local custom. It was a huge rambling place, as she remembered it, that had been in the Bruce family for hundreds of years, passed on from father to son.

During her last visit, ten years before, the old house had been in the hands of Irwin Bruce, and Tarin's recollection of him was somewhat vague, but she had no such difficulty remembering his son Darrel. Now that she was back she found it rather

6

embarrassing to remember the number of times she had sought excuses to be in certain places at just the right time to catch a glimpse of Darrel Bruce and, even in the brief time she had been back, she had several times wondered if she had been foolishly impulsive in coming back.

It was not as if she had ever been on even remotely close terms with him—all her adoration had been from afar, but during the long summer days when she had been on holiday from school, he had seemed like the very essence of romance to her young eyes.

Perhaps if she had suffered some disillusionment at his hands during those days she would not have retained such a glowingly romantic picture of him. As it was whenever she recalled him to mind he appeared as the perfect figure of all a man should be, and it only now began to occur to her that such a paragon could not possibly exist among the everyday male population. In all probability he had changed as much, or more, than she had herself during the passing years.

Usually when she had seen him he had been out riding and he had greeted her politely, though never as warmly as she wished, for she had nursed a youthful crush that had caused her both agony and ecstasy. Once, she recalled, she had returned from a long walk quite lightheaded with delight, and all because, after finding her with a painfully twisted ankle, Darrel Bruce had brought her all the way back from Stonebeck, riding on the saddle in front of him.

She had seen neither Deepwater nor Darrel Bruce for more than ten years now, but she admitted, though only to herself, that it had been the idea of actually working for him that had prompted her to write for the post of secretary, and travel all the way from the south of England for an interview.

The casual reference to it by her uncle had sent her, without mentioning anything about it, to buy a copy of the Scottish paper that contained the advert, although she had some difficulty in obtaining one. For several hours she had mulled over the idea and finally decided that there could be no harm in applying, even if she was wasting her time.

Her parents had been curious as to her reasons, but they had said little, for they never interfered with her plans, and she had told them that she liked the idea of working in Scotland and of seeing her uncle again. Robert had been glad to see her and she had no doubt that she was welcome to stay as long as she liked. Tomorrow was to be the big day, and she felt quite suddenly nervous of meeting her youthful heart-throb again, although she told herself more than once that it was quite probable he wouldn't even remember her existence.

'Nothing seems to have changed.' she said, smiling at her uncle. 'It all seems so much the same, so ageless and so incredibly big—even now I'm grown-up!'

'Now you're grown-up,' her uncle echoed, and there was a hint of amusement in his expression that made her frown briefly.

She was always being told that she looked a lot less than her years and she did not always take it as a compliment. 'I'm twenty-four, Uncle Robert,' she reminded him, and he smiled.

'And showing no sign of settling down to marriage?' he said in the accent she always found so attractive and which had all but disappeared from her father's speech after so long away. 'A girl as pretty as you are, Tarin, shouldn't be thinking of nothing but her work. Have you no plans for marrying and settling down, lassie?'

'Oh, I've one or two boy-friends,' Tarin told him offhandedly. 'Quite a few, in fact.'

She was reluctant to have the subject of marriage discussed, for it was something that her parents often mentioned, indirectly when she was there and more openly when they thought she was out of earshot. So far she had met no one who came close to her idea of a husband—not, that is, since the days of her childhood when she had indulged in secret dreams of becoming Darrel Bruce's bride and living at Deepwater. It was a fancy that now brought a flush of embarrassment to her cheeks when she even thought about it.

'No one serious?' her uncle asked, and she shook her head.

'No one serious, Uncle Robert.'

Robert McCourt frowned for a moment, then leaned across the table and touched her hand lightly, a half-apologetic look on his face. 'Tarin,' he said quietly, 'would you think me vain if I asked you to call me just Robert and dispense with the Uncle?'

Tarin smiled and shook her head. 'No, of course I don't,' she told him. 'I always call my other uncles by their christian names. It does make you sound a bit ancient, doesn't it?'

'It makes me feel older than I am,' Robert admitted with a grimace, 'and that's not good for my morale.'

'It's funny,' Tarin mused, looking at him with her head to one side, 'you've changed a lot more than Deepwater has. You look a lot younger than when I saw you last.'

His laughter made him appear even more youthful and Tarin was glad to see it, for there had been a long time when he had become so morose and uncommunicative, after Aunt Margaret's death, that the family had worried about him. It was good to see him laughing again, even if it was at what she said.

'You've grown up in the time, lass,' he told her. 'I wasn't so very old, you know, the last time you were here, but you were only a wee bit of a thing, no more than twelve or so.'

'Actually I was fourteen,' Tarin told him with a smile. 'But I can see what you mean—everyone looked much older to me then, of course.'

Her uncle looked at her for a minute without speaking, then he gave his attention to the coffee she had made for them, not looking at her when he spoke. 'And now you're wanting to work for the Bruce,' he said quietly.

Tarin had guessed he wouldn't be very happy about it, but so far he had said nothing, and she had hoped to keep it that way. Robert had never been away from the Highlands in his life, unlike his brothers, and he still held his views, firmly steeped in ancient history. The ancient feud, the tradition that the McCourts and the Bruces never mixed, still mattered to him.

'It sounds like a good job,' Tarin said, sounding as matter-of-fact as if she knew nothing about past history. 'The pay's very good and I couldn't resist the temptation to come up here and live—if I get the job, of course. Darrel Bruce might not consider me suitable for it.'

'And why would he not?' her uncle demanded. 'You're a good worker, I've no doubt of it, and a McCourt's good enough for a Bruce any day! If he doesn't——'

'Robert!' Tarin put a restraining hand on his arm. 'I don't want to rekindle the old feud! There's really no need for you to get up in arms about it before it happens, or even if it does. I shall apply for the job in the usual way, and if Darrel Bruce doesn't think I'm suitable for it he'll no doubt say so and there'll be no hard feelings.'

'Indeed there will!' Robert declared stoutly. 'Though you'd probably be like Douglas and let it ride—you're too much like your father, lassie, he never was a fighter!'

Tarin laughed, not so much at her uncle, but at the idea of his still keeping up the old feud between the Bruces and the McCourts which had gone on, in some form or other, for over two hundred years. 'Robert!' she said, shaking her head at him, 'I won't have you going out for Darrel Bruce's blood just because he turns me down for a job! It's —it's idiotic after all these years!'

Robert McCourt's eyes looked bright and indignant and she realised ruefully just how serious it was to him. 'It's something you wouldn't understand,' he told her quietly. 'You don't belong here like I do, Tarin, you'd not see things in the same way.'

'Then you mustn't blame me for wanting to work for the Bruce,' she said, using the local name for the head of the Bruce family. 'If I get turned down, well——' She shrugged, then looked out of the window again to where the huge bulk of Deepwater was hidden in its surrounding trees, just beyond the village to which it gave its name. 'But I'm hoping I won't be turned down,' she added softly.

'They say Darrel Bruce is a hard man,' her uncle told her, still taking the pessimistic view. 'Though he seems to be well liked enough in the village. They say he's hard to please and ready to turn anything to money, though he can't be in such dire straits, with all the things he's done there since his father died.'

It was difficult to be casual about her interest, Tarin recognised, and it was amazing how she still felt a small tingle of excitement at the mere mention of Darrel Bruce. 'Did he have a hard time after his father died?' she asked, and her uncle nodded.

'So I heard,' he said. 'Though he seems to have that great place working well for him now, by all accounts—even if it does mean the whole place being overrun with American tourists!'

'Well, it is a hotel,' she reminded him with a smile. 'That's what his letter said, although the job itself isn't only concerned with that side of it.'

Her uncle's eyes narrowed and he looked at her for a moment almost suspiciously. 'Of course you'd need to correspond with him, wouldn't you?' he said, as if the idea had only just occurred to him. 'Did he remember you?' he asked, and Tarin shrugged, wishing she knew the answer to that herself.

'I shouldn't think so,' she said with deceptive carelessness. 'He didn't say he did, and after all this time it's quite possible he's forgotten I ever existed!'

'Aye, well——' Her uncle nodded, as if such a thing was quite feasible, and Tarin felt a twinge of disappointment. Some reassurance from him would have been welcome on that point.

'Anyway, he'd never recognise me now,' she said, and again her uncle nodded.

'You've grown into a very lovely young woman, Tarin,' he told her. 'No one can deny that—and they do say the Bruce has a taste for lovely girls.'

'Not surprising,' Tarin commented, hoping her voice sounded more offhand to him than it did to herself. 'I expect we've all changed, even Deepwater, now that it's a hotel.'

'Not so much a hotel, so I hear,' her uncle told her, 'as a kind of country club, or whatever it is they call those places. The Americans stay there more like private guests, though I've no doubt they pay well for the privilege of it.'

Tarin looked out again at the concealing trees that surrounded Deepwater and hid the old house from her view. The smile that touched her mouth was because she recognised her uncle's apparent dislike of the American visitors as merely an extension of his feeling for their host.

'Deepwater's a lovely old place, from what I remember seeing of it,' she said. 'I imagine the visitors think it well worth while paying a bit extra to stay there.'

'They drive their great cars through the village as if the devil was in the back seat,' Robert declared, determined not to relinquish his prejudices. 'The village isn't the same at all since he turned that place into a business.'

Admitting to being somewhat biased in the opposite direction, Tarin smiled. 'Anyway, I should think it's better than simply sitting back and going bankrupt,' she said, and her uncle looked at her for a moment in silence, evidently recalling something to mind.

'You were keen on young Bruce when you were here before, were you not?' he asked then, and Tarin was appalled to find herself blushing, something she had thought herself grown out of. It seemed that no matter what vows she made to treat past emotions as mere childish folly, she was still vulnerable, and that blush made it obvious.

'I remember having a childish crush on him at one time,' she admitted, and laughed as if such things were well in the past. 'Don't forget I was only fourteen the last time I was here and he would be about twenty, I suppose. He cut a very romantic figure in my eyes then—now I'm older and so is he, I'll probably hate the sight of him. Especially if he's the hard man you say he is.'

Her uncle shrugged. 'Some women find a hard man more attractive, so I've heard,' he told her, and Tarin recognised the truth of that with a brief nod, trying to remember exactly what it was she had so admired in Darrel Bruce before.

He would, she hastily worked out, be about thirty years old by now, and the wonder was that he was not married yet. Presumably he wasn't, for her uncle had not mentioned it, only that he had a taste for pretty women. Not that she had any thoughts at all on the subject, but briefly her childish fancies took a whirl into the realms of possibility.

'Oh, I don't think you'll hate the sight of him,' Robert told her with a certain gloomy satisfaction. 'He's a good enough man to look at, and he's not short of opportunities with all those wealthy American women always around.'

'Any one in particular?' Tarin asked casually, and he shrugged as he helped himself to more coffee.

'There's talk in the village that one young woman's got her eye on him,' he told her with a dash of coarseness that brought a smile to her lips. 'Gloria Stein or some such name—but whether it's just a rumour of something more than that, well——'

'Gloria Stein?' Tarin puzzled over the name for a moment. 'That name seems to strike a note—I believe there was a girl called Gloria used to ride with him when I was here last.'

She recalled, though only vaguely, a tall and rather haughty blonde girl who used to ride a lot with Darrel Bruce but had never quite been able to keep up with him, much to Tarin's satisfaction at the time. Surely if she was still coming to Deepwater after ten years, there must be something serious.

'She's quite a looker, from what I've seen of her,' Robert McCourt told her. 'Though she's a wee bit brassy for my taste and I'd say he has his hands full with her if I'm any judge, she looks a hard case.'

'Then they should make a good pair,' Tarin said, smiling ruefully. 'And I must say you're not painting a very rosy picture for me, Robert. You really don't want me to work for him, do you?'

She was smiling as she asked the question, and possibly her uncle didn't realise just how serious she was behind that smile. Had she really made a big mistake in coming back to Deepwater? Could it all be so different that she wouldn't even like it here any more? From what she could see, the place was as lovely as ever it had been, but she now had

15

some doubts about the old house and its residents.

Whether Darrel Bruce had changed the old place into something she would neither recognise nor like. Whether its mellow stone face had been lifted and prettied up to suit American visitors, and its lovely grounds scarred with swimming pools and tennis courts to amuse the wealthy tourists. It was a sobering thought and she didn't think she could face seeing it again, if it had changed so much.

'I'm not trying to put you off working for him, Tarin,' her uncle told her earnestly. 'I'd like nothing better than you staying on here with me—I'd love your company.'

'Then just keep your fingers crossed that I get the job,' Tarin told him with a smile. 'I don't ever remember when I was so nervous about going for an interview, and I can't think why I should be.'

Her uncle's brown eyes looked across at her speculatively for a moment as he studied her in silence, then he nodded and smiled. 'You'll be woman enough to stand up to yon Bruce now,' he said with evident satisfaction. 'You'll not let him browbeat you, I know, and you'll have that job!'

'I hope so,' Tarin said quietly, and looked again at that screening cluster of trees that hid Deepwater from her view. 'I really do hope so.'

The sky had a curiously luminous look where it sat on top of the distant hills as if some great light shone just out of sight and was reflected in the blue morning sky. There were clouds, but only the little white streaks like puffs of smoke blown slowly along on the light breeze. It was a beautiful morning and Tarin chose to see it as an omen.

16

She was walking through the village, relieved to find it unchanged since her last visit ten years before, and she would almost have sworn that even the packets and tins in the grocery shop window were the same ones. The little houses were just as neat and sturdy, set in their small patches of gardens and the twisty road still looked bumpily cobbled in the morning sun as she clicked her way over them towards the clustering trees that surrounded the entrance to Deepwater's carriageway.

One or two people recognised her, and probably knew of her coming from her uncle, for he was not averse to an occasional gossip. They looked no older and she forgot for a moment that she herself looked vastly different from the fourteen-year-old that most of them remembered.

Ten years ago she had been thin to the point of scragginess and her face had had a small, soulful look that was appealing if not actually pretty. Now she was a young woman, still small in stature, but no longer thin, nicely rounded and exquisitely shaped, flattered by the thin, best silk dress she wore that fluttered round her slim legs as she walked. Her face was still small, too, but more than merely pretty, and the big dark blue eyes only faintly apprehensive as she faced the prospect of meeting Darrel Bruce again after so long.

She remembered him so clearly it was quite amazing. The times she had seen him, usually mounted on that big grey mare of his, and looking even taller than he was in fact, his reddish-brown hair thick and wind-tossed above that broad brow, his brown eyes alert and eyeing her curiously. Probably wondering how she came to be always around whenever he was out near Stonebeck or Torin's

17

Pool, probably seeing through her ruse and quietly amused by it.

As she left the village behind and approached the carriageway, she felt her heart doing a rapid and quite distinct flutter against her ribs and she put a hand to her side and frowned. It was really quite idiotic of her to behave like a lovesick schoolgirl after all this time.

The gravel crunched under her feet and she found herself hurrying, walking right in the middle of the wide drive, as if she felt safer there than near the overhanging trees. It was because her heart was beating so hard and she was so preoccupied with thinking about her youthful memory of Darrel Bruce that she heard nothing of anyone approaching until a voice yelled from behind her and a loud whinnying sound sent her spinning round, her eyes wide with surprise.

A bend in the drive had hidden her from the view of the approaching horseman and he had had to take swift and violent avoiding action to prevent his mount knocking her down. The horse, a dark brown stallion that looked as vast as a house from Tarin's viewpoint, took an extremely poor view of being pulled up and made to swerve so sharply and he was giving his rider a hard time handling him for the moment.

'What the hell are you walking in the middle of the road for?' the man demanded, his hands busy with the indignant animal, and an edge of violence on his strong voice. 'You almost threw me!'

'I'm sorry!' Her heart was hammering hard at her ribs, and it was not simply with the startling effects of the horseman's sudden appearance either. She had no doubt at all that she was apologising to what she had hoped was her future employer, and if his present mood was anything to judge by, she had just banished any hope she ever had of getting the job.

The horse steadied at last and the rider gave his attention to her, his strong hands still holding a tight rein on his mount, brown eyes looking down at her curiously. He said nothing for a moment but studied her with an intensity that brought the colour to her cheeks in resentment of it. It was not the reaction she had expected from her first sight of Darrel Bruce after ten years of seeing him as her ideal man, and she realised that she had been right to think she would think differently about him now she was grown up.

There was no doubt at all that he was attractive, as her uncle had implied, but he had an arrogance about him that she did not remember noticing before. His thick reddish-brown hair still looked as if he had been riding fast and disturbed any sort of grooming it might have had initially, but there was a rugged, angular look about his features that made no pretence of being good-looking.

Light fawn trousers fitted his long muscular legs closely and were tucked into short shiny brown boots, a fawn shirt had its sleeves rolled up to above the elbow and exposed strong, suntanned arms that looked both sinewy and powerful and an open neck showed a column of brown throat and neck as strong and dark as mahogany. He was, she realised with a slight dizzying sensation in her brain, even more potent than she recalled, despite her resentment of his manner.

'You're Tarin McCourt?' he said, and made it a statement rather than a question.

She nodded and put a hasty hand to smooth her hair, somewhat disconcerted at having him arrive so unexpectedly and so alarmingly. 'Yes,' she said, and he half smiled.

It was little more than a faint glitter in those brown eyes, but it was warmer than the darkly angry look she had first encountered there, and she took hope from it. 'You've changed,' he said frankly, and Tarin flushed.

'So have you,' she retorted swiftly.

His laughter was unexpected, and she felt a small shiver slip along her spine at the sound of it. Sitting up there on that great stallion he might have been the same ancestor who snatched Jeanie McCourt from the bosom of her family over two hundred years ago and started that never-ending feud between the two families.

'One of the battling McCourts!' he said with a hint of a jeer, and Tarin looked up at him indignantly.

'I haven't come to do battle, Mr. Bruce,' she said in as steady a voice as she could manage. 'I came to see you about a job, if you remember.'

'So you did.' He sat looking down at her for a second or two while the stallion stirred restlessly and tried to toss his head, prevented by the firm hold on the reins. 'Are you on your way up to the house?' he asked, and Tarin nodded.

'I was, yes.'

'Changed your mind?' he asked swiftly, detecting the tone of voice she used as being doubtful.

Tarin stared at him for a moment, then shook her head. 'No, Mr. Bruce, I haven't,' she told him. 'I came all the way up from the south of England for this interview, I shan't change my mind now.'

'You really want to work for me?' he asked, and she hesitated, wondering if this wasn't a rather too unconventional place for an interview.

'I like the sound of the work,' she said cautiously, putting it on a less personal basis than his question made it sound.

'What about me?' She could have sworn there was a hint of faintly malicious laughter in his eyes again as he looked down at her, and she hesitated, but briefly.

'Oh, I think I could cope,' she said with a far more offhand air than she felt, and he smiled openly this time.

'Oh, you do?' he said softly, and pulled his restless mount round firmly, the powerful muscles rippling in those long legs as he kept control. 'Well, report to me in the morning at nine sharp,' he said, and Tarin stared for a moment, only finding her voice when he put his heels to his mount and clucked him into action.

'Mr. Bruce!'

He pulled the animal up sharply again and turned to face her, a small impatient frown between his dark brows. 'What is it?' he asked, and Tarin sought wildly for words for a moment as she stood there on the wide carriageway, her head spinning with the speed of it all.

'How—I mean—just like that?' she finished lamely, and he frowned again.

'Is there anything else?' he asked shortly. 'You don't need references about my character, do you?'

'No, of course not, but you might——'

'I know you!' he told her impatiently. 'I don't need to ask a whole string of questions about you. You're a McCourt, and they're honest enough even

21

if they are as prickly as hedgehogs about everything under the sun.' The brown eyes swept down the slim, rounded length of her and back again to her flushed cheeks. 'You're pretty enough not to make the place look like a morgue and you say you're a good secretary, what more do I need? If you want the job be here in the morning, if not——' Broad shoulders shrugged carelessly, then he laughed shortly. 'You'll be there!' he guessed confidently, and Tarin had no time to retort before he turned his mount yet again and was riding hard and fast along the curving drive to the house, leaving her staring after him in something of a daze.

CHAPTER TWO

IT was difficult trying to explain to her uncle about the unconventional nature of her interview with Darrel Bruce, and Tarin thought he was highly suspicious about the whole thing, despite her reassurances. He had said surprisingly little, however, and she wondered if Darrel Bruce's remark about the McCourts being honest, if nothing else complimentary, had pleased him in some odd way. For herself she was still horribly uncertain and not nearly as confident as she assured her uncle she was. In fact she viewed her return to Deepwater this morning with as much trepidation as she had yesterday.

It was a lovely, mellow day and the hills had a misty look as if the sun was already drawing a veil over them from the water in the network of rivers and lochs that enclosed this beautiful, wild country. It had never failed to enchant her when she was a rather romantically inclined schoolgirl, and she felt no differently now.

The village cuddled close to the protective sweep of Torin Brae, small and sleepy in the morning sun and backed by the tree-girt mass of Deepwater. She had always wanted to see the inside of the old house, but now that the opportunity was there she was having doubts. Although, if she was honest, all the doubts concerned the unexpectedly arrogant master of Deepwater, not the house itself.

She let her mind dwell again briefly on Darrel Bruce, but found the thought too disturbing for early morning peace of mind and hastily dismissed it in favour of choosing what to have for breakfast. Her uncle admitted to being a very inexpert cook, despite several years as a widower, and he had readily accepted her suggestion that she should do the cooking, something she quite enjoyed.

Bacon, eggs and sausages, perfectly grilled and fried, were received enthusiastically by her uncle, and she hoped the rest of her day would go as well as the start. She was somehow not very confident that it would, but set off after breakfast in high hopes and much more nervous than she admitted to.

The short half-mile or so walk between her uncle's house and the village gave her the opportunity not only to admire the scenery but to think as well, and she almost laughed aloud in disbelief when she recalled how offhandedly she had been given the job she had travelled so far for.

She had expected the usual confrontation across a businesslike office desk, with a more mature version of the quiet and rather serious young man she remembered as Darrel Bruce. Instead she had been almost run down by a fiercely short-tempered and arrogant creature riding an animal that looked as spirited and volatile as its rider. No request for references, which she was willing and able to produce, no formal interview or discussion of pay and conditions—nothing but a swift and disconcerting exchange with a man who was even more disturbing than she remembered him.

The mellow golden-blue sky did a lot to lift her spirits as she neared the village, and she looked across to where Stonebeck lay like a hollow green bowl with a stream running like a silver ribbon through it. It was a beautiful country and she certainly looked forward to living there, no matter what disturbances occurred from time to time.

She could imagine that working for Darrel Bruce, as he was now, would be a far from tranquil experience, but there would always be the compensation of living and working in beautiful surroundings. Blue skies, misty green and purple hills and valleys and silver-brown water—it was all so lovely and also slightly unreal somehow, but she loved it.

She passed the first of the cottages that marked the beginning of the village and walked the narrow road with an easy stride, one thumb hooked in the shoulder strap of her handbag, and marvelled at the stillness. Then, almost as if to prove how wrong she could be, the strident blast of a car-horn blared suddenly at her around a bend in the twisting little street. Remembering the incident of yesterday when she had nearly been run down by Darrel Bruce and his mount, she stepped hastily to one side and pulled a wry face. It was more dangerous walking in this quiet Scottish village than in the busy town she was more used to.

The car that sped past her was huge and shiny and a bright flame colour that looked garish in the early sun, and she just caught a glimpse of the driver as blonde and female before the whole noisy *ensemble* disappeared around the next bend, its horn still blaring. It was no doubt one of Darrel Bruce's rich American visitors, and she found herself wondering just how much contact she would have with the people who stayed at Deepwater.

She exchanged greetings with a couple of people who recognised her and made her way through the village and on to that long curving carriageway that led to Deepwater. Her heart, she was dismayed to find, was already beating with excessive force against her ribs as she faced the prospect of meeting Darrel Bruce again, and she despaired of her own foolishness.

There was nothing outwardly different about the old house, she was relieved to see, although she thought it looked rather less run down than it had in Irwin Bruce's time. But there were no tennis courts or swimming pool that she could see, just the same wide, stone-flagged terrace with its worn steps and a stretch of green lawn between the house and the gardens.

The heavy dark wooden doors had the same forbidding look she remembered from the old days, but one of them was ajar and she sighed with relief at not having to use the enormous iron bell ring that was set in the wall. It was a kind of hotel now, she reminded herself, so it was hardly likely that the doors would be closed against callers, but she was thankful just the same. In the old days the sight of that huge iron ring always made her shiver when she imagined it producing a great clanging of bells somewhere in the depths of the old house.

Having climbed the stone steps she opened the door a little further and stepped inside, gazing round, quite startled at what she saw. With the idea of a hotel firmly fixed in mind she had expected the usual foyer atmosphere, with a reception desk and the customary furnishings and staff on hand.

Instead there seemed to be no one but herself around and the huge, stone-flagged hall might never have changed for a hundred years or more. Faded banners hung from the walls and iron torch brackets waited for flaming torches to be put in them to flicker brightly and illuminate the high cloister-arched ceiling and the off-white walls.

There were dark, sombre paintings too, of past Bruces, with their strong, rugged features and hair much more red than the present descendant's was. Fierce, ruthless men who hadn't been restrained by modern manners and laws; men like Duncan Bruce who had stormed the McCourt household and carried off the fair Jeanie.

In her own mind she had often wondered if Jeanie McCourt, all those years ago, had been as unwilling a bride as the McCourts always claimed. There had been rumours that she had been having a secret love affair with her abductor, and Tarin had always preferred to think that was the case; seeing Darrel Bruce yesterday had made her even more certain. Mounted up there on that great horse, he had looked perfectly capable of carrying off any woman he took a fancy to.

Jeanie Bruce, as she became, had borne four lusty sons, who in turn had laid the foundation for the next generations, but unfortunately their descendants had been less productive, and Darrel was now the only survivor, apart from some distant cousins in Australia or somewhere, so she'd heard. It would be sad, she thought, if a proud old family like the Bruces were to die out, and she once again began speculating about Darrel and the American woman he was supposed to be interested in.

'He isn't there, he's in the dining-room!'

Tarin spun round sharply, eyes wide, her expression almost guilty, although she had been doing no more than a little private speculation. 'Good— good morning,' she said shakily, and eyed him warily.

He was, almost inevitably, dressed for riding, she did not remember ever seeing him dressed any other way, and it certainly suited him. The blue shirt he wore this morning seemed to emphasize that deep tan, and gave his features an even craggier look. He was also much taller than she had realised, well over six feet, she guessed, and his hair *was* almost as red as his ancestors' when he stood in the sun as he did now, looking at her with one brow raised and a hint of impatience in his expression.

'You were looking at the portraits,' he said. 'But you won't find Duncan there, he has pride of place in the dining-room.'

He told her that last as if he was daring her to say anything about the past history that still could cause a rift between the two families. Her uncle had never spoken to a Bruce in his life and probably never would. Thinking the whole thing rather silly in the present circumstances, Tarin smiled and pulled a face.

'It's all rather ancient history, isn't it?' she said, and was quite surprised when he frowned.

'You don't carry on the feud?' he asked, and Tarin shook her head.

'I shouldn't be here if I did, Mr. Bruce.'

His wide mouth quirked briefly into an answering smile and he put a hand under her elbow and turned her towards a door at the far end of the hall. 'I'm rather surprised you are, to be quite honest,' he told her. 'I'm sure your uncle doesn't approve, does he?'

'Not really.' She admitted it reluctantly, for she had no desire at all to start off on the wrong foot.

'But I'm the one who wants the job, not my uncle.'

'And you really think it will be worth coming all this way for?' he asked as he opened the door and ushered her into the room in front of him.

Tarin hesitated, then nodded. 'I hope so,' she said, and looking around her, wondered if it really would prove to be worthwhile. Deepwater itself was somewhat overpowering, and Darrel Bruce was much more of an unknown quantity than she had expected him to be.

The room was not particularly big, but it was well in keeping with the character of the house that she had seen so far. That great hall and the rugged air of grandeur about the whole place. It was high-ceilinged and more oblong than square, with an earthy, primitive kind of beauty that was difficult to specify.

The walls were white, as in the hall, with black, heavy wooden beams spanning its ceiling and a huge bay window with small diamond-patterned panes. The furniture was sparse but suitable for an office, and all of it beautifully polished and preserved, including a massive walnut desk behind which was a modern leather-upholstered swivel chair that looked perfectly in keeping.

Another, smaller desk stood in the curve of the great bay and Darrel Bruce indicated the chair behind it with a casual hand. 'Sit down,' he invited.

Tarin did as she was bid and looked around her curiously. It was quite unlike any office she had worked in before, but presumably this was where she would be working if she kept the job. 'It's a lovely room,' she ventured, attempting to break into the silence that was beginning to make her uneasy because she was aware that he was watching

29

her, and at any moment she was going to blush like a schoolgirl and feel a complete and utter fool as a consequence.

'I'm glad you approve!' She might have been wrong to attribute sarcasm to the reply, but she bit hastily on the retort that rose to her lips and instead simply looked up at him enquiringly.

'Mr. Bruce, if you——' she began, but he took no notice of her attempted interruption.

'You've never been here before, have you?' he asked, and she shook her head.

'No, never.'

He had perched himself on the edge of the desk, close enough for her to be uneasily conscious of his presence, and she could feel her pulses racing blindly, almost in panic, as she hastily looked down at her hands again to avoid those intently steady eyes. It was almost as if she expected him to make some sudden and unexpected move towards her, and that idea was quite ridiculous in the circumstances.

Then he smiled and she sensed it even before she glanced up at him again. 'It must have been very much slower in my younger days than my notorious ancestor was,' he said quietly, and Tarin bit her lip, that dreaded blush staining her cheeks without her being able to do a thing about it.

It was quite idiotic to colour like a schoolgirl just because he paid her an indirect compliment, especially when he was probably quite practised in flattery with so many wealthy female visitors to please. She should have had more control, but during her working life she had worked for a variety of employers and never one as able to make her feel gauchely uneasy as Darrel Bruce did. Without quite knowing why, she began to resent it.

'You were hardly likely to notice me then, Mr. Bruce,' she said with studied quietness, and swept her long lashes up to look at him for a moment steadily, her heart hammering hard at her side. 'I was only fourteen the last time I was here and you were much more mature.'

He looked at her for a moment, narrow-eyed, and she wondered if she had been too rash. 'Not so much more, surely,' he said quietly, in that firm, deep voice. 'I must have been about twenty, and my tastes haven't changed that much!' His eyes glinted maliciously bright for a moment as he eyed her from head to foot. 'But don't worry,' he added softly, 'I have far too much on my mind to spend time chasing my secretary around the office, however stunning she might be!'

Tarin gasped audibly and tried to object. 'Mr. Bruce, I——'

His eyes glittered at her darkly and there was a hint of cruelty, she thought, in the way his mouth quirked at one corner. 'You can assure your uncle that there's no chance of history repeating itself!' he said.

Tarin was too breathless to reply at once and she sat there behind the desk while he perched beside her with one foot swinging. He seemed impatient and angry for some reason she could not quite fathom, and it was disturbing, too, to her own peace of mind, the way his being so close could affect her. She despaired of ever being able to think about Darrel Bruce sensibly, for that schoolgirl crush would keep getting in the way.

Determinedly she controlled her voice and tried to sound coolly efficient. 'I'm hoping to work for you, Mr. Bruce,' she told him quietly. 'Nothing else has even entered my head, I can assure you!'

For a moment he said nothing, then he laughed, a short, hard sound, and slid from the edge of the desk to stand over her, one hand on the back of her chair. 'It entered *my* head the minute I saw you on the driveway yesterday,' he confessed frankly. 'I think our mutual ancestor, the bonnie Jeanie, must have looked like you—that's why old Duncan ran off with her!'

'Don't you know?' Tarin retorted swiftly. 'I'd have thought you knew as much or more about her than we do! After all, she spent most of her life as a captive at Deepwater!'

'A captive?' It was obvious the idea amused him. 'You've a very dramatic turn of phrase, Miss McCourt! Duncan chose a quite common way of taking a bride—quite permissible in his day and age!'

'To people like the Bruces, maybe!' Tarin retorted. 'But it still means she was a captive!'

'A bride,' he insisted, those brown eyes glinting. 'She was a bonny girl and he wanted her, so he took her. After all, the Bruces were the local top dogs, it was quite an honour for her in a way.'

'An honour?'

He nodded, his eyes challenging her to deny it. 'She seems to have realised it too,' he said. 'In all she lived at Deepwater for about forty years, and she never, as far as we know, made any attempt to run away.'

'Would she have dared?'

His laughter was warm and deep and the sound of it ran through her like a shiver, then he leaned forward and briefly she was enveloped in a spicy, masculine scent that tickled her nostrils pleasantly.

'She would have if she really *was* anything like you,' he told her. 'And I think she must have been to have caused such a furore.'

Tarin's heart was fluttering wildly, no matter how she tried to control her reactions, but she met his eyes with deliberate boldness. 'You must know,' she said. 'If she spent so much of her life here, surely there's a portrait of her too.'

He shook his head and there was a glint of what could have been malice in his brown eyes as he looked down at her. 'She was still a McCourt, for all Duncan fancied her,' he said coarsely. 'She was never painted, even though all her sons were.'

'Oh!' She looked at him for a long moment, then shook her head slowly. 'Poor Jeanie,' she said softly. 'Loving a man who saw her only as a mother to his sons.'

Darrel's eyes quizzed her, and he put a hand on the back of the chair behind her, a movement that brought him even closer so that she was once more aware of the warm, male strength of him. The broad chest and sinewy arms that half enfolded her with that curved arm. 'Who said anything about love?' he asked softly.

Tarin did not quite know where to look, and her heart was hammering away like a steam hammer as she sought for words to explain. 'I—I've always thought perhaps she loved him,' she said in a small husky voice. 'I mean, staying so long and—I always hoped she did, it wouldn't have been quite so bad for her then, would it?'

He said nothing for a while, then he shook his head and she realised suddenly that he was laughing to himself, his brown eyes glittering with amusement as he considered the idea. 'You *are* a romantic, aren't you?' he said, still laughing. 'I'd never thought of bringing love into the old family story, but do you know, you could just be right. Maybe Duncan did love her, I wouldn't know, I've always taken it at face value and not bothered about the niceties of it.'

'Just like a Bruce!' Tarin retorted sharply, without knowing why she was suddenly taking up the old feud again when she had vowed not to. She flicked him a hasty look through the thickness of her lashes and shook her head. 'I'm—I'm sorry, Mr. Bruce.'

'Are you?'

He was still bent over her and she wished he would stand up and give her senses a chance to get back to normal, but he was speaking again and his breath stirred the silky hair on top of her head. 'I said you were a battling McCourt,' he said softly. 'And it looks like I was right, doesn't it?'

'I'm sorry.' She looked up at last and met the direct gaze of his brown eyes only inches above her. 'I didn't intend to even mention that silly feud,' she said a little breathlessly. 'I vowed I wouldn't—I can't even think how people can keep up a quarrel about something that happened over two hundred years ago!'

'Easy,' Darrel said with a malicious smile. 'We do it instinctively!'

She sat for a moment giving it some thought, and wondered if this was a sample of what could happen over and over again if she worked for him. 'If you—I wonder if you'd like to reconsider, Mr. Bruce,' she said at last. 'I mean, if you'd rather have someone else for a secretary—I'll—I'll understand if you've changed your mind.'

'I haven't.' He straightened up for a moment and then almost at once bent over her again as he searched her face with bright glittering eyes. 'Have you?' he asked softly.

It was doubtful if he saw her shake her head, for the door behind him opened at that moment and someone came in. It was not possible for Tarin to see who it was at first because he blocked her view, but when he straightened up and turned to speak to the newcomer, she recognised the blonde woman who had passed her, driving that flame-coloured car at such breakneck speed. She was as sure as she could be that it was the same one, and she saw the narrow-eyed way she was looking at her and then at Darrel Bruce.

It was quite possible, of course, that his attitude of being bent over her had given the wrong impression altogether, and Tarin's heart was rapping at her ribs in agitation when she saw the malice in those pale blue eyes. Then she came further into the room, a tall, smooth woman with boundless self-confidence, except probably when it came to being sure of Darrel Bruce, and there she was suspicious and uncertain.

'I wondered where you'd got to, Darrel,' she said in a flat voice. 'Aren't we going riding this morning?'

She came across to the desk, long legs encased in skin-tight cream-coloured trousers and short brown boots, a blue silk shirt almost matching his and making her pale blue eyes look even sharper. She held her gaze on Tarin as she came and Tarin looked down at her hands, wondering what would happen when she knew he intended taking Tarin into his employ. She would not like the idea, it was obvious, and Tarin saw no conceit in understanding her reasons.

'I had an interview first,' Darrel said. 'I told you that last night, Gloria.' He looked back at Tarin and waved a large hand in her direction. 'Miss McCourt, this is Miss Stein, one of our guests—Miss McCourt is my new secretary, Gloria.'

'McCourt?' The pale eyes narrowed again and she looked at Tarin suspiciously, ignoring the hand she proffered. 'Say, isn't that the name of——'

'An ancestor of Miss McCourt's,' Darrel told her with a grin. 'The hatchet is about to be buried after more than two hundred years!'

'Oh?' There was no hint of friendliness there, and Tarin had an uneasy feeling that if Miss Gloria Stein had her way, the hatchet would be other than buried. 'Well, how long does it take to interview a secretary, for heaven's sake, honey?' she asked Darrel, and pushed a possessive arm through his, smiling up at him blandly. 'Aren't you coming with me?'

'Give me ten minutes,' Darrel told her with a brief frown for her persistence. 'Now let me get on, Gloria. The sooner you get out of here and let me set Miss McCourt to work the sooner I'll be able to join you.'

Gloria Stein's blue eyes again looked at Tarin, narrowly suspicious, and the rather tight mouth had a faintly sulky look, but she yielded to his firmness without argument. 'O.K.,' she allowed reluctantly 'But don't be too long, honey, or I might just go without you!'

For a brief moment he held her gaze steadily, then Tarin saw the way she hastily looked away and felt almost sorry for her. 'You won't,' he said with quiet certainty, and gave his attention once more to Tarin while Gloria Stein turned without saying another word and went out of the room.

Tarin felt embarrassed for the American woman and wished she need not have witnessed her brusque dismissal. Gloria Stein, she thought ruefully, would make a bad enemy, and if she was to work for Darrel Bruce there would be plenty of cause for Gloria Stein to regard her as an enemy. There were already far too many complications to the situation, and she felt suddenly quite sure that she should never have applied for this job in the first place.

Darrel Bruce was likely to prove the most discomfiting man she had ever worked for, and she wished she had the strength of mind to speak out now and tell him she was going back home—that she had changed her mind. Instead she knew in her heart she would stay because no matter how many years had passed, or how much he had changed, he was still Darrel Bruce, and he could still do things to her senses that no other man had ever done.

She blinked at him suddenly when she realised he had spoken to her, and she had not even heard what he said. The brown eyes were regarding her curiously and one dark brow was raised in query. 'I asked if you were ready to start,' he told her, and she hastily brought herself back to earth.

'Oh, yes—yes, of course, Mr. Bruce! I mean,' she amended hastily, 'I shall have to give notice to my last firm, of course, but I'm on holiday for the next two weeks, so if you want me to start now, I can.'

He stood beside the desk, towering over her, his hands on his hips, a faint look of resignation on his face as he looked down at her. 'All of which boils down to the fact that you *can* start now,' he guessed dryly, and she nodded.

'I'll ring my present—my last firm and tell them I've found another job up here,' she said. 'I couldn't tell them before I came away because I didn't know if you'd give it to me.'

Slowly the brown eyes moved over her, their expression bright and quite blatantly appreciative, then he smiled. 'Do you ever have trouble getting jobs?' he asked softly, and she hastily avoided looking at him.

'I haven't had many jobs,' she told him, trying to sound cool and calm when her heart was hammering at her breast. 'I went straight into one from secretarial school and I've changed about three times since then.'

'Then you'll know that very few men would turn down the opportunity of having you around the office,' he said with embarrassing frankness. 'You must have known I'd take you on, Miss McCourt, so why be coy about it?'

'I'm *not* being coy!' Tarin denied indignantly. He really was the most uncouth man at times, and she again had thoughts of telling him she had changed her mind.

'No?' He shrugged after a moment or two, and shook his head. 'You've got the McCourt prickles, anyway,' he told her tactlessly. 'And if you really want to work for me you'll have to learn to keep your temper. I'm not an easy man to work for, but I know my shortcomings, and if you don't like what's in store for you, you'd better go now, while you're still in one piece!'

Tarin's chin was angled defiantly and her eyes sparkled with determination as she looked up at

38

him. 'Don't worry about me,' she told him. 'Just tell me what you want me to do and I'll get on with it.' She opened the top drawer of the desk and took out a shorthand notebook and pencil, wondering briefly as she did so what had happened to her predecessor. 'Did you want to dictate?' she asked.

He shook his head, regarding her for a moment as if he was trying to assess just how much she would take without telling him what she thought of him. 'Not right away,' he told her. 'I presume you know how to file letters? It might help if you started on that and felt your way around, find out where everything is, before I start you on the real work. You'll find the files in the usual system and you have access to all the cupboards, etc., except my private desk. Anything from the accountants comes direct to me, everything else you can go through first and then simply give me the ones I'll need to attend to personally. O.K.?'

'Yes.' She was more than ready to be left on her own, even if it was simply to get her breath back and get her bearings.

He still stood beside her, looking down, a small frown on his brows. 'You're sure you've got the idea?' he asked. 'Say so if you haven't, don't just go blithely on and leave me in a state of chaos!'

Tarin flushed, her eyes sparkling again with anger at the suggestion that she was less than capable of coping with a few bits of filing. 'I'm a trained secretary, Mr. Bruce,' she told him in a cool voice, her chin angled as she looked at him down the length of her small nose. 'I'm quite capable of doing a simple job like filing letters!'

It was bound to amuse him, of course, her indignation, and she knew he was laughing to himself even though it showed only in the bright glint of his eyes. His face was set soberly as he nodded his head. 'Then I'll leave you to get on with it,' he told her. 'If you need anything during the next half hour or so, just hang on until I get back—nothing will collapse in that time!'

She nodded without saying anything and he walked across to the door, turning to look at her for a second before he went out. He looked serious and quite stern for a moment when she glanced at him, but then one eyelid lowered briefly and expressively in a broad wink, and she caught a glimpse of white teeth in the tanned ruggedness of his face before he turned and left the room.

CHAPTER THREE

TARIN thought her first day at Deepwater had gone rather well considering all things, and she hoped it would prove to be an omen for the rest of her time there. As it turned out she had seen very little of Darrel Bruce for the rest of the day, and she was uncertain whether or not she was pleased or sorry about it.

The half hour or so that he had predicted he would be gone with Gloria Stein had in fact stretched on until nearly lunch time and Tarin had taken advantage of his absence to do some tidying up—something her predecessor had either omitted to do, or had no time to do before she left.

There was, she soon discovered, more than one firm of accountants with whom he corresponded at some length, and she had carefully separated their letters and statements from the less confidential mail. There was even one firm who wrote from America, and it surprised her to learn that his interests were so widely scattered.

His private desk she left strictly alone, as she had been instructed to do, and she did no more than add to the pile of letters already there and awaiting his attention. She had no difficulty finding enough to keep her busy, for the filing basket had been piled high with an accumulation of correspondence. With plenty of time on her hands she had had the opportunity to clear it all long before he returned and also to do some general tidying up.

With the sun shining in through her bedroom

window the following morning, she faced her second day at Deepwater with much more confidence, although it also brought to mind the question of how she would get to work when it was pouring with rain, as it was prone to do in this part of the world, even in summer.

The walk through the village and along that lovely tree-lined carriageway was delightful when the weather was fine and bright, as it was now, but it would be a lot less attractive a prospect during bad weather, and that was something she would have to consider.

She had never driven a car in her life, but perhaps now was a good time to learn, for she could scarcely expect her uncle to turn chauffeur on her behalf every time the weather changed. It was something she must consider quite seriously. With the generous salary that Darrel Bruce would be paying her she would soon be able to afford a small car and the problem would be solved.

She was still mulling over the question of learning to drive as she made her way down the carriageway, some time later, and she brought herself swiftly back to earth when she heard a vaguely familiar sound on the gravel behind her. It took her a moment or two, but she eventually recognised it as the sound of galloping hooves and, remembering how Darrel Bruce had almost run her down the day before, she moved hastily to one side out of danger.

Expecting him to appear at any moment round the bend in the carriageway, as he had yesterday, she was dismayed to find that the pulse at her temple was suddenly much more rapid, and she put up a hand instinctively as she turned, a greeting ready on her lips. It was something of a surprise when she failed to recognise the rider and she stared at him for a moment in wide-eyed astonishment.

It was not Darrel Bruce but a thinner and more boyish-looking man, who eyed her with some interest as he came nearer and smiled broadly at her expression. He reined in his mount when he drew level with her and she thought there was something elusively familiar about his features, but as yet she could not place them.

She responded willingly enough to the smile because he so obviously meant to be friendly. 'Hello there, did I scare you, coming up behind you like that?'

The accent was unmistakably American, and she immediately put him down as one of the visitors to the hotel. She smiled and shook her head, standing well back from the horse that was not quite as big as Darrel Bruce's massive stallion, but equally as restless.

'Not at all,' she assured him. 'I was—I was just expecting someone else, that's all.'

'Oh, I get it—you were surprised, not scared.' She nodded and he swung himself down from the saddle, falling into step beside her as she walked on. She was not unwilling to be friendly, but she hesitated about being too responsive because as yet she had no idea what her new employer's feelings were about his staff mixing with the guests, and this man was presumably a guest.

He was quite attractive too, in a fresh-faced, boyish way. Medium tall and wirily thin, he was well tanned, as if he spent a good deal of time in the open air, with thick, short-cropped brown hair that grew back from a broad forehead, and grey eyes that beamed at her appreciatively above a wide white smile.

'I haven't seen you around before, have I?' he asked, and Tarin shook her head.

'I only started here yesterday,' she told him. 'I work for Mr. Bruce—I'm his secretary.'

'You don't say?' His mouth pursed in a silent whistle. 'Say, Darrel sure has some luck, doesn't he?'

'Does he?' She smiled her appreciation of the compliment, and he nodded earnestly.

'Sure he does if he has you for a secretary!' He rolled his eyes heavenwards, smiled again, then proffered a hand. 'I'm Con Stein—Conrad Stein third to be formal, but I hope we won't be formal. I'm Con to my friends!'

Tarin's hand was gripped in a clasp that was unexpectedly firm and strong and she found herself smiling in response to the almost boisterous friendliness of him. It occurred to her as well that the vague familiarity of his face was explained by his name. He must be related in some way to Gloria Stein—probably he was her brother.

'I'm Tarin McCourt,' she said.

'Tarin?' He repeated her unusual christian name as people often did on first acquaintance, then nodded approval. 'Say, I like it, it's pretty!'

'I was introduced to a Miss Stein yesterday morning,' she said. 'Would that have been your sister perhaps, Mr. Stein?'

'You met Gloria?' He looked vaguely surprised for a moment, then smiled knowingly and nodded his head as he pulled a wry face. 'Yes, if you were with Darrel, I guess you would see Gloria around,' he added.

He was almost embarrassingly frank, and perhaps not quite as naïve as he appeared, but Tarin liked him instinctively. There was something refreshingly open about him that appealed to her, unlike his more sophisticated sister whose manner had been anything but friendly.

'I *was* with Mr. Bruce,' she agreed. 'I was being shown what to do—being my first day.'

Her companion raised a surprised brow. 'And Gloria chipped in?'

'Not really,' Tarin said hastily. 'Miss Stein came to see if Mr. Bruce was ready to go riding with her.'

He nodded, that same knowing look in his eyes. 'She would!' he said, and pulled another wry face. A moment later he looked at her and laughed engagingly. 'I guess you think I'm pretty much of a heel, talking like that about my sister, huh?' he guessed. 'But—well, Gloria's just Gloria, I guess, and I know her pretty well. She isn't so bad really, and maybe I shouldn't malign her the way I do!'

'It's a brother's privilege, isn't it?' Tarin smiled.
'I guess it is at that!'

He seemed quite uninhibited and not at all reticent about talking to a complete stranger about his sister's shortcomings, but Tarin wondered what Gloria Stein would have said if she had been a witness to it. 'Are you on holiday here, Mr. Stein?' she asked, seeking a more safe subject than the possessive blonde who had seemed to look upon Darrel Bruce as her own personal property.

Tarin barely noticed the brief hesitation before he answered, and there was nothing suggestive of reticence in the broad smile he turned on her. 'I guess you could say we are,' he told her. 'We spend quite a bit of time here one way and another.'

'I could be quite wrong,' Tarin ventured after a

moment or two, 'but I seem to remember a Miss Stein staying at Deepwater when I was here last—about ten years ago.'

'Could be,' Conrad Stein said. 'We've been coming here since the year dot, our families have always been friends.' The look in the friendly grey eyes was frankly appraising and he smiled. 'The way things are going,' he added with a grin, 'I think I'll come even more often. The scenery's certainly improved a lot!'

'It's a beautiful old place,' Tarin said, deliberately misunderstanding, although she was not at all averse to the flattery.

'Great!' he agreed with a grin. 'And it's got a terrific history, you know.'

Tarin smiled wryly. 'Yes, I know!'

For a moment he walked beside her in silence, as if he was suddenly preoccupied, then he looked down at her, frowning curiously. 'Your name kind of rings a bell,' he told her, 'though I can't for the life of me think why. I've never met you before, I'm sure of that, or I wouldn't have forgotten you!' He shrugged. 'Oh well, I guess it doesn't matter, I've met you now. How come you're back here now, after ten years, Miss McCourt?'

Tarin shook her head, not prepared to give her true reasons and hesitant about giving others. 'It just seemed like too good an opportunity to miss,' she told him with a smile. 'I've always loved it here, when I used to stay with my uncle and aunt, and the chance to work here was too much.'

'You don't live round here?' he asked, and she shook her head.

'I suppose you could say I do now,' she said. 'My father comes from here, but we've lived in Surrey all *my* life.'

His frown was plainly curious. 'And you came back here just to take a job with Darrel?' He shook his head, as if her reasons were beyond his understanding. 'Well, I guess you know what you're doing, and you look sane enough not to be dazzled by those caveman tactics!' He caught her puzzled look and laughed. 'I'm just kidding, Miss McCourt,' he said. 'Darrel's O.K.!'

They had walked almost as far as the house and were just turning the last corner in the curved carriageway, the trees shushing softly overhead in the morning breeze. The gravel surface crunched flintily under the horse's hooves and made the loudest noise to be heard in the still of the morning as he plodded patiently beside his erstwhile rider, and there was a stillness and tranquillity about the whole place that gave Tarin a sudden sense of wellbeing. It was just like coming home, she reflected, and started visibly when Conrad Stein suddenly snapped his long, bony fingers together sharply.

'*Now* I know where I've heard your name before,' he said. 'The legend—the story of the feud between the Bruces and their near neighbours, I remember now. Her name—the one who was carried off by one of the Bruces, was Jeanie McCourt, wasn't it?'

'That's right.' Tarin found herself unwilling to discuss the matter of the feud, and the act that had started it, with a stranger. Perhaps because she had, in her own mind, compared the current master of Deepwater with his disreputable ancestor, and found it too discomfiting to wonder how much further the comparison would go.

'A taboo subject?' he guessed, one brow elevated

47

curiously. 'Sorry, Miss McCourt, I guess I shouldn't have mentioned it.'

'Oh, it doesn't matter in the least,' Tarin assured him hastily, not wanting to make a mystery out of it as well as a legend. 'After all,' she added with a laugh, 'it *was* more than two hundred years ago!'

'All those old legends fascinate me,' Conrad Stein confessed. 'And especially when they concern people I know, or at least their ancestors. In this case I now know both sides of the battle!'

'It's ancient history,' Tarin reminded him. 'Best forgotten except as what it is—an old story, probably well trimmed in the process of being handed on!'

As they approached the old house it looked so bland and mellow in the morning sun that Tarin found it hard to believe it had housed such a fierce and reprehensible family as the Bruces of Deepwater once were. They came to a halt at the foot of the worn stone steps that led to those massive doors and once again Conrad Stein proffered his hand.

'I guess I have to hand you over to Darrel now,' he said with obvious reluctance. 'I sure hope I see you again, Miss McCourt.'

'I hope so, Mr. Stein.' She took the proffered hand and made no objection when the long, thin fingers held hers for longer than was strictly necessary. 'Thank you for walking up with me.'

He laughed as he swung himself back into the saddle, ready to ride round to the stables at the back of the house. 'Oh, Darrel doesn't have the monopoly on chasing beautiful women,' he informed her, and urged his mount forward, waving one hand as he went. 'So long, Miss McCourt, I'll be seeing you!'

Tarin pondered as she went up the steps to the house just what her new acquaintance had implied by his last remark. Twice during their conversation he had made allusion to Darrel Bruce's prowess with women, and her uncle too had implied that he had a taste for pretty girls. He had even said as much himself.

At first glance he gave the impression of being much too stern and uncompromising to be a ladies' man, but even a few moments with him gave the lie to the idea. He was a very attractive man in a ruthless kind of way, as her own response to him proved. It was after all a very long time since her last sight of him, but she had no hesitation in admitting that her schoolgirl crush was far from being banished altogether.

When she opened the door of the office they shared she found Darrel Bruce already there, and she glanced at her wristwatch as she turned to close the door behind her. She was not late, but nicely in time, which was how she liked to be, but seeing him there made her wonder if he was one of those men who liked their staff to arrive early.

He seemed to look even taller this morning, she thought, and dismayingly stern and discouraging. Fawn slacks and a shirt of the same colour fitted snugly to his long, sinewy body and gave him an earthy, sensual look that she found alarmingly disturbing, despite his apparent aloofness.

His thick hair, so nearly red like his rampaging forebears, still looked wind-tossed, as if he had come there straight from his morning ride, and there was a hint of frown between his dark brows. He stood behind his desk and glanced up when she came in, nodding his head but showing no sign of a

49

smile on those strong, craggy features.

'Good morning!'

The greeting was brusque and barely polite, but she attempted a smile when she replied, then, discouraged from verbal pleasantries, walked across to her desk and took the cover off her typewriter, ready for work. If he preferred to be silent first thing in the morning it was all right with her. In fact in the circumstances she preferred it too, for she found his presence there so soon rather disconcerting.

It gave her no time to settle in, even to check and see if she needed any minor repairs to her hair and make-up. Instead she was faced with the need to cope with a quite alarming disturbance in her pulse rate, caused by seeing him there. Somehow, and soon, she must stifle that schoolgirl idiocy once and for all.

'Did you notice a letter from a New York firm when you were filing yesterday?'

The question was so sudden and unexpected that for a moment Tarin looked at him rather vaguely, then she shook her head. 'I don't remember one,' she said, and walked over to the filing cabinets lining one wall, confident of her filing system. 'If you tell me the name of the firm I can find it for you.'

'It shouldn't have been in your hands,' he said shortly. 'But try under Lucas while you're there, I can't find it under Fennelly.'

'Fennelly and Lucas,' she said instantly, and smiled. 'You'll find it under the papers on your desk, Mr. Bruce.'

'Oh?' His brown eyes narrowed suspiciously. 'How do you know that?'

Surprised by his tone, she blinked for a moment,

'Why, I put it there,' she said, and he frowned.

'I thought I made it clear,' he said coldly, 'that my desk was out of bounds—now you tell me you've been going through the papers on it.'

'I did no such thing!' Tarin denied indignantly, stung to anger by the accusation.

'No?' One dark brow lifted as far as the thick hair over his forehead. 'Then how else do you know where that letter is?'

Tarin took a deep breath, trying hard to control a temper that was rapidly getting out of hand, but determined to show nothing but contempt for his behaviour. 'I found the letter lying on the floor,' she said quietly. 'It was obvious it had blown down from your desk and, being flimsy paper, it was quite likely to blow down again if I simply put it back on top. So I raised the pile and slid it underneath!'

He said nothing, but lifted the pile of papers on his desk and sorted them through from top to bottom until he found the missing letter. Without saying a word to her, he read it through, then sat down at his desk and began to make notes on a pad in front of him.

Tarin stared at him for a moment, her anger churning away inside her until she could resist it no longer. She looked at him down the length of her small nose as he sat behind the desk, veiling the look in her eyes with the thickness of her lashes.

'I'm not in the habit of spying on my employers, Mr. Bruce,' she told him in a small, tight voice.

He looked up swiftly and there was a glint of puzzled amusement in his eyes that made her wonder if his short temper of a few minutes ago had been her imagination. 'Are you spoiling for a fight?' he asked softly, and Tarin hastily looked away again, curling her fingers into her palms. It was infuriating how hard she found it to outface him, even when he was in the wrong.

'No, of course I'm not!' she denied firmly.

He leaned back in his chair, swinging it back and forth on its swivel as he spoke, his brown throat exposed when he tipped back his head to look up at her standing on the other side of his desk. 'Of course you're not!' he mocked, still in that same soft, taunting voice. 'You want me to apologise, is that it?' he asked, and Tarin did not answer. 'Well, Miss McCourt?' he prompted gently.

'You did accuse me,' Tarin said huskily, and he smiled.

His long fingers were steepled under his chin, his elbows resting on the arms of his chair, and the brown eyes watched her steadily from under half-closed lids. It was a slow, slumbrous and infinitely sensual gaze that sent little shivers of sensation along her spine like icy fingers.

'Let's get something straight, shall we?' he said softly. 'I'm not an easy man to work for, I admit it without qualification, but I *am* the boss around here, no matter what anyone else says or does. Deepwater is mine and if you want to work here you'd better realise from the word go, that what I say goes; what I do is my affair and no one else's. Maybe you find my manners not up to your requirements, but frankly that doesn't concern me one bit, Miss McCourt, I don't set out to please anyone!'

'Not even your paying guests?' Tarin retorted, without stopping to think that she might be treading on thin ice.

She thought he resented her reference to paying guests, for there was a dark, angry look in his eyes for a moment before he replied. 'The guests are no concern of yours,' he informed her bluntly. 'I've had no complaints so far.'

Tarin could well believe it, but she was unwilling to admit as much, and she felt an almost irresistible need to dig even further. 'They wouldn't dare!' she retorted, and was somewhat disconcerted when he laughed.

He got up from behind the desk and her heart gave a sudden lurch of panic, although heaven knew what she expected him to do. Half the craggy face was in shadow and his eyes glinted at her darkly from below the dark brows.

'I knew you'd come out fighting,' he said, his wide mouth crooked into a smile. 'Any other female would either have burst into tears or walked out and given up, but not you! Not one of the battling McCourts!'

It was a much more personal argument suddenly but far removed from the original cause. Tarin's Scottish ancestry might have been submerged for most of her life, but at this moment it was uppermost, and the ancient feud was as real to her as it was to her uncle. She was determined not to let this ill-mannered, arrogant creature get the better of her and she stuck out her chin, her eyes sparkling and deep blue.

She was for the moment Jeanie McCourt, battling against her captor's determined efforts to subdue her, and she realised with a start that Jeanie's reactions were probably very much the same as hers were to Darrel Bruce. It was neither hate nor love that she felt, but a strange and disturbing

53

mixture of both, combined with an instinctive desire to resist, and it made her tremble like a leaf as she faced him across the desk.

Then she gave herself a swift, mental shake and looked at him as coolly as her churning emotions would allow. 'Is that what you're trying to do, Mr. Bruce?' she asked in a betrayingly shaky voice. 'Make me give up the job?'

'No.'

The short, and apparently truthful answer gave her a moment's hesitation, then she shook her head. 'Then if——'

'Is it what you want to do?' he countered, and the erratic stirrings that steady gaze aroused in her almost blinded her to the fact that she was shaking her head.

'No, of course not!' She shook her head even more vehemently and was quite sure she meant what she said, no matter how angry he made her.

A trace of laughter still lingered in his eyes and he folded both arms across the broadness of his chest while he looked at her. 'You promise to do as you're told and not start a fight every time I give you an order?' he asked softly, and Tarin flushed at the obvious effort to anger her again.

'I'll do my job to the best of my ability, Mr. Bruce,' she said quietly. 'I've never had any complaints about my work or my behaviour from other people I've worked for. If you'd looked at my references——'

A large hand dismissed such ideas contemptuously. 'I don't need references, I prefer to trust my own judgment,' he told her, 'Especially somebody I've known all my life.'

Tarin blinked, startled to notice how intimate

54

the words sounded. 'Have you?' she asked huskily, and her eyes were wide and very deep blue as she looked across at him. 'Known me all your life,' she explained when he looked briefly puzzled.

'It seems as if I have,' he said seriously. 'And I know the reputation of the McCourts well enough, you may be touchy, but you're honest and——'

'It didn't sound as if you thought so, just now!' Tarin retorted, unable to resist it, but a large hand dismissed her objection.

'Touchy, as I said,' he repeated, 'but honest enough. I remember you when you were at school,' he went on, blandly unaware of the curl of embarrassment she experienced when she was reminded yet again of her own youthful folly. His brown eyes looked across at her steadily and there was a glint of malice in their depths, she would have sworn. 'You always seemed to be around,' he said.

'Only for three or four weeks in the summer,' Tarin said, refusing to look at him. 'When I was on holiday from school.'

'Was that all it was?' he asked apparently surprised. 'I thought you were here all summer, you seemed to be about for a long time.'

Instinctively she was on the defensive again, her eyes bright with embarrassment for her youthful adoration of him, knowing he must at last be aware of her discomfiture and hating him for adding to it. 'I'm sorry I got under your feet,' she said shortly, not stopping to choose her words. 'I was only a schoolgirl and not very bright when it came to hero-worship!'

She had not meant to be quite so frank about it, to confirm what he must have already been pretty sure of, but it was out now and there was a glint in

55

his eyes that recognised her slip and enjoyed it.

'So you *did* have a schoolgirl passion for me?' he said softly. 'I thought it must be that because you always happened to be at the same spot I happened to be.' His gaze slid slowly over her from the top of her head to the soft curves that showed above the edge of his desk. 'What a pity it's worn off,' he added even more softly, and flicked a dark brow upwards. 'Or has it?'

Tarin caught her breath, not knowing whether she was more angry or embarrassed. She had never in her life had to cope with a man as devastating or as unnerving as Darrel Bruce and she found herself at a loss to know what to say or do next. Her more usual self-confidence seemed to have deserted her for the moment and she felt again like that adoring, tonguetied schoolgirl.

'I—I wish——' she began, and licked her lips nervously. 'Mr. Bruce, I want——'

'Now you're not going to change your mind and walk out on me after all, are you?' he asked, his eyes gleaming, and she shook her head, her spirit roused again by the suggestion that she was running away.

'Oh no, I'm not going to let you drive me to the point of walking out,' she told him in a small, determined voice. 'If you want to get rid of me, Mr. Bruce, you're going to have to sack me, and that could cost you money for wrongful dismissal!'

He stared at her for a minute in silence, as she stood small and defiant facing him across the big desk, then he threw back his head and laughed. It was a full, deep sound that did strangely disturbing things to her pulses and she clenched her hands as she stared at him, unsure just what to make of her own reactions. Then he leaned forward and rested his hands on the top of the desk until his face was only inches from hers.

'So you'd sue me, would you?' he asked softly.

Tarin angled her chin defiantly. 'I would—you deserve it!'

The brown eyes glittered at her darkly and she could feel her heart hammering furiously hard in her breast as she held his gaze for as long as she could. 'I believe you would,' he breathed softly at last, and reached out with one hand to touch her cheek with his fingertips, a touch that was almost sensual in its gentleness. 'You'd better watch your step, Tarin McCourt,' he said in a deep, quiet voice. 'You might have met your match!'

CHAPTER FOUR

THE next three weeks seemed to go by in a dream for Tarin, although she was kept busy enough. She had not realised just how much correspondence was involved in running a hotel, and she took quite a lot of dictation every morning, not all of it to do with the hotel.

Darrel Bruce seemed to have a lot more business interests than she had realised and, judging by the brief glimpses she had of the mail, most of them were profitable. After what her uncle had told her about his financial straits after his father's death, she could not help but admire his subsequent efforts to put things right.

One of his greatest admirers was Mrs. Smith, the housekeeper. She had been housekeeper at Deepwater during his father's lifetime and when the house became a hotel had remained with Darrel to act in a similar capacity. She was a gentle but firm-willed old woman and she and Tarin had hit it off from the beginning.

She stood no nonsense either from the guests, whom she was inclined to regard as interlopers however wealthy they might be, or from the staff under her command, and the smooth efficiency with which Deepwater was run was a credit to her methods. Darrel Bruce was the only man she seemed to stand in awe of, and to some extent Tarin could understand that, for he was a man not to be taken lightly in any capacity.

It was the housekeeper who saw to it that Tarin

had her coffee just the way she liked it, and it was she too who revealed the reason for her predecessor's departure. Apparently the poor girl had been unable to stand her employer's impatience with certain discrepancies in her work and she had departed one day in tears.

'She'd not the stamina for the work,' Mrs. Smith had declared, and gave the impression that she expected better of Tarin.

It was Mrs. Smith who was responsible for Tarin getting her first glimpse of Duncan Bruce too, although in the circumstances Tarin was doubtful about the wisdom of taking such liberties in the absence of her employer. 'Won't Mr. Bruce object?' she asked as she followed the indomitable old lady to the huge room that had once been the banqueting hall and now served as dining-room for the hotel's guests.

'Don't worry,' Mrs. Smith assured her. 'After all, you've a right in a way to see the man. He was connected with your family too.'

'I suppose so,' Tarin allowed uneasily, and paused in the doorway to gaze around her.

She had never seen any of the other rooms at Deepwater, and this one was unexpectedly impressive. It was, she suspected, unchanged since Duncan's day except for certain refinements, concessions to modern comfort which wealthy visitors would expect. But in character it had changed little.

The room was huge with massive beams supporting the arched ceiling in an intricate and deceptively delicate pattern. White walls gave it a cool and rather stark look and were hung with innumerable portraits of past Bruces, all of them having

59

that distinctive red hair and fierce dark eyes. Most of them were bearded and looked wild and arrogant enough to overawe anyone, especially a young, seventeen-year-old girl like Jeanie McCourt had been at the time of her abduction.

'Yonder he is,' Mrs. Smith told her, and indicated a portrait hung immediately above the huge fireplace. Her shrewd eyes studied Tarin's reaction for a moment. 'He's a braw man, is he not?' she asked softly.

Tarin stood in silence for a moment, unable to speak because her heart was beating furiously hard and making her breathless. Duncan Bruce, the man who all those years ago had snatched a young girl from her family and started a seemingly endless feud, looked down at her from his ornate gilt frame and it was almost like recognising someone she had known all her life.

Brown eyes, alarmingly familiar, had a bright, challenging look and his jaw, only poorly disguised by a fierce red beard, thrust out as if in defiance of her opinion, or anyone else's. His hair was red and thick and fell partly over a broad brow in a way she was familiar with in another face, and Tarin found she was smiling to herself.

'Is he what you expected?' the housekeeper asked, and watched her closely as she put the question.

Tarin nodded. 'Exactly as I expected,' she said with a hint of irony. 'Take away that beard and you have the present Bruce—yes, he's exactly as I expected him to be.'

'He was a fine man, was he not?' Mrs. Smith pressed for further approval, and it was obvious that she too saw the resemblance to her employer in the painted features of Duncan Bruce, hence her admiration.

'Physically he obviously was a fine man,' Tarin agreed readily enough. 'But his morals surely left much to be desired, didn't they?'

'That's a harsh judgment!'

The voice behind her was unexpected and Tarin swung round hastily, a breath caught in her throat. Her reaction was, she recognised, only partly due to being caught by her employer in the act, so to speak. Her heart was thudding wildly in her breast and she felt herself between two stools, with Duncan's portrait glowering down at her from one side and his equally disturbing descendant on the other.

Mrs. Smith was smiling tolerantly, not in the least alarmed at being discovered by him in the act of showing his secretary around the house when she should have been working. 'I'd a mind to show Miss McCourt the portrait, sir,' she explained. 'I knew you'd not mind.'

'Not in the least,' Darrel agreed, and perched himself on the edge of the huge table that ran half the length of the room.

Cream trousers fitted closely to his long legs and a white shirt revealed powerful brown arms below the short sleeves. A glimpse of tanned flesh showed where the open neck gaped across his broad chest, and Tarin wondered rather dazedly if he ever did more than casually comb his thatch of reddish hair.

His brown eyes had the same bright, challenging look as those of the man in the portrait, and Tarin felt an involuntary shiver slip along her spine when she met their gaze briefly. Her knees were trembling and she told herself she was behaving quite idiotically in the circumstances.

'What do you really think of him?' he asked quietly, and she shook her head uncertainly.

'You'd scarcely expect me to be an admirer, would you?' she asked.

'I don't see why not,' Darrel told her. 'After all, he's over two hundred years old now, and most of our female visitors seem to find him quite—attractive.'

Tarin met his eyes again briefly, aware of the housekeeper watching with interest and showing no sign of returning to her own duties, even though her employer obviously meant to carry on as guide.

'They can probably see the likeness to you, that's why,' she replied, and only realised how her words could be interpreted when she saw the way one dark brow flicked upwards into that thick swathe of hair across his forehead.

'A compliment?' he suggested softly, and the brown eyes were bright with laughter.

Tarin shrugged with exaggerated carelessness, and again met his eyes for a moment. 'If you like,' she said. 'I don't imagine you suffer from any false modesty, Mr. Bruce.'

'Would you want me to?'

The words were a definite challenge and Tarin looked uneasily at the housekeeper before she answered. Yet again she could feel herself getting out of her depth with him, and she was reluctant to have Mrs. Smith's shrewd eyes witness her obvious discomfiture.

'In the vernacular,' she said in as cool a voice as she could summon, 'I couldn't care less what you do, Mr. Bruce.'

Her reaction had been sheer defensiveness, noth-

ing more, and she already regretted it, as she so
often did on these occasions. For a moment he said
nothing, but she had seen the swift, dark glitter
that came into his eyes, and the tightening of his
mouth.

'You just can't resist it, can you?' he said softly.
'You're as determined to keep it up as your uncle
is!'

'I didn't mean——'

'You meant me to be put firmly in my place!'

He interrupted her relentlessly, and Tarin felt a
small cold, shrinking sensation in her stomach.
Even Mrs. Smith showed resentment for her manner, and her round, homely face showed plain indignation that her employer should be spoken to in
such a way.

'If you'll excuse me, sir,' she said with a brief,
disapproving look at Tarin, 'I'll away back to my
work.'

'You do that, Mrs. Smith!' He spared the housekeeper a glance and a reassuring grin, then turned
his attention to Tarin again. 'I can take care of
Miss McCourt.'

Mrs. Smith's shrewd old eyes had a definite glint
in them when she looked at him. 'Aye, sir,' she said
quietly, 'I've no doubt you can.'

Left alone with him, Tarin was appalled to find
herself so nervous that she licked her lips with the
tip of her tongue and held her hands clasped
tightly together. For a long time the brown eyes
studied her, then he smiled. 'Well,' he said, 'shall I
sack you for insubordination, or let you get away
with it?' He laughed softly, then reached out and
touched her cheek. 'I'm a fool,' he said softly, 'but I
think I'll keep you.' Her attempted interruption

he silenced with a finger to her lips. 'Don't,' he said.

The rest of the staff worked longer, but Tarin worked only a five-day week and she made the most of her free time. Sometimes she felt rather as if she was on holiday, although she worked so hard, and there always seemed to be new places to discover and new things to do. She had even toyed with the idea of learning to ride so that she could get further afield, but so far she had done nothing more constructive than think about it.

She shopped at week-ends in Gillespie, the nearest town, and some time, of course, was spent doing household chores, for her uncle was not the most domesticated of men and willingly left it all to her. She was an excellent cook and they lived well, for her uncle had a small but thriving engineering business in Gillespie, so there was no financial strain.

As she had done each Saturday since her arrival, while her uncle was at the office she cleaned the whole house through ready for the week-end, but attempting to do that and at the same time keep an eye on a fruit cake she had made for Sunday tea was bound to prove disastrous. And so it was, though not quite in a way she could have anticipated.

She had decided to give the fruit cake another minute or so, so she left it to go and finish some dusting in the small sitting-room at the back of the house. It was several minutes before she looked at her watch again and she had just decided that disaster was imminent if she didn't go at once, when the door bell rang.

With her hair tied back with a spotted blue scarf

and her slim figure enveloped in a huge yellow apron that had once belonged to Aunt Margaret, she clucked her annoyance at the interruption as she went to answer the summons. There was a hint of flour from her baking on the tops of her bare arms too, although heaven knew how it had got there, and she brushed at it absently as she went to the door.

Finding Darrel Bruce there was a distinct shock and she stared at him for a moment with wide, disbelieving eyes, her lips parted in surprise. For a moment the brown eyes looked at her, a hint of disbelief in their depths, then he smiled and Tarin felt her heart start up a clamour in her breast, though she condemned herself for a fool for allowing him to affect her so violently, simply by smiling.

A pale blue shirt showed off that mahogany dark tan to advantage and was open far enough down from the neck to show the smooth dark shadow of his chest. Dark blue trousers hugged his lean hips and clung to the long muscular legs, his feet planted firmly apart on the red-tiled porch floor.

'Good morning,' he said quietly, and shot one brow into the thick hair over his forehead. '*Are* you the lady of the house?'

'I suppose you could say I was,' Tarin said, rather shortly, for she imagined a slight in the question, mostly because of that raised brow. 'Can I help you, Mr. Bruce?'

'Actually I wanted to see your uncle,' he told her, and Tarin blinked her surprise. She had never known her uncle have anything at all to do with the Bruce family, and she could hardly believe he would willingly do so now.

'He—he's not here at the moment,' she said, her reaction plain on her face. 'Is it important? He's at the office, but he'll be home in about another hour or so.'

'Not so important it won't wait another hour,' he said, and sent a swift appraising glance over her from that concealing scarf over her dark hair to the low-heeled shoes she wore. 'I'd never have seen my very efficient Miss McCourt as a domesticated creature,' he told her in a soft and very provoking voice, and Tarin was dismayed to feel the flood of colour that warmed her cheeks.

Maybe it had something to do with that very personal 'my', but she wished suddenly that she was more presentable. Being seen in an apron several sizes too large for her and with her hair bundled up in a scarf would not have been so important if the caller had merely been a casual tradesman, but to have Darrel Bruce see her looking like that was disconcerting to say the least.

She put up a hand and swiftly snatched the scarf from her head, letting the long thick silkiness of her hair swing down over her shoulders, shaking her head in a gesture that was partly defiant. 'I'm sorry I look such a mess,' she said in a betrayingly husky voice, 'but I wasn't expecting callers, and especially not you.'

He leaned himself against the jamb of the door with one long arm stretched upwards so that his hand touched the top of the frame, and looked at her for a moment in silence. But there was some inner glow that lent warmth to those brown eyes and gave her a strange curling sensation in the pit of her stomach.

'I'm not complaining,' he said softly. 'But you do

look *very* domesticated.'

'And you don't like domesticated women!'

The retort had been defensive, almost instinctive, and she saw the way his mouth tightened and the way his long body tensed suddenly as if he resented the retort. He straightened up and stood squarely facing her in the narrow confines of the little porch, his expression stern and unfriendly, and she felt an immediate regret for having brought about the change.

'I don't know whether it's because you think you know me, or simply a natural cattiness that makes you say that,' he told her coolly. 'But I refuse to rise to your bait, Tarin!'

It was the very first time he had called her by her first name, and it would have to be in anger, she thought ruefully, shaking her head over her own impulsiveness. 'I—I'm sorry,' she said.

He continued to look at her steadily for a second, then seemed to make up his mind about something. 'If I thought you meant that,' he said quietly, 'I'd ask to come in and wait until your uncle comes home. As it is I'll come back later and see him.'

'Oh, please!' She looked up at him appealingly, appalled to think that he thought her so inhospitable. 'Please come in and wait,' she said, looking almost tearful in her earnestness, and stood back, holding the door wider in invitation.

For a moment she thought he was going to be persuaded and come in, but then he shook his head and a wry smile just touched his wide mouth as he turned away. 'No, thanks, Miss McCourt, I guess maybe the hatchet isn't as firmly buried as I thought. I'll call back and see your uncle when he's home.'

'Oh, but what shall I tell him?' she called as he went down the short front path in long-legged strides. 'Why do you want to see him?'

He turned when he got to the gate, and one brow lifted for a second, making comment on her change of manner. 'I'll discuss that with your uncle,' he told her. 'That is, if he isn't too proud to do business with a Bruce!'

'I—I wish you'd wait.'

Her voice was wistful now, and she was quite unconscious of looking as soulful as she did, standing there in the doorway wrapped in the folds of that outsize apron. She bit her lip anxiously when he turned again and her eyes were as wide as a child's, making her look much less than her years, meeting his gaze head on despite the more rapid state of her pulse.

Without another word he turned again and strode back up the garden path and she stood back, holding the door wide a tentative smile on her face. She indicated that he should precede her along the short hall way, but instead he made her go first, his fingertips just touching her bare arm where the flour smudges still showed white on her soft skin, and she breathed a sigh of thankfulness that she had finished in the sitting-room before he came.

The little sitting-room always looked bright and sunny, and particularly so now when it smelled of lavender polish, and the furniture gleamed from her recent ministrations, the cushions on the settee freshly plumped. She indicated that he should sit down, and despaired of her own weakness when she realised the way her legs were trembling.

Seated on their rather small settee he looked taller

than ever, and sat with his elbows on his knees, leaning forward slightly. He looked just as much at home in the tiny sitting-room as he did in his own more palatial quarters, and she realised that he was a man who could adapt himself to almost any surroundings quite easily.

'Can I—would you like some coffee?' she asked, and he looked at her with a hint of a smile for a moment before shaking his head.

'No, thank you,' he said solemnly. 'And please don't let me interrupt your work—I'm sure you must be busy.'

'Oh, I've finished now,' she assured him. 'I left this room until last so that I could keep an eye on the——' She put a hand to her mouth in dismay when she remembered her reason. 'Oh no!' she said despairingly. 'My cake!'

Ignoring his politely raised brows, she dashed into the kitchen and flung open the oven door, making a small heartfelt moaning sound when an ominous charring smell tickled her nostrils. A thin wisp of dark smoke wafted out with the rush of heat that flushed her cheeks, and she could have cried to think what he must be thinking of her domestic skills.

'Is it very bad?'

He must have followed her into the kitchen and he stood in the doorway just behind her when she turned a flushed face and suspiciously bright eyes to look at him. The nicely risen but too dark fruit cake sat in the oven looking horribly uneatable, and Tarin felt as if she could have burst into tears there and then.

'It's burnt to a cinder!' she moaned dismally, and without thinking put her hands into the hot oven to take out the baking tin.

Her cry of pain coincided with the thud of the cake tin and its contents as they hit the floor and scattered charred crumbs in every direction. She was aware of him striding swiftly towards her as she thrust her stinging fingertips into her mouth instinctively, only to make the pain worse.

'Don't do that!'

He snatched her hands from her mouth and held them for a moment in his, looking at the moist red and sore tips, then he reached for a clean dry tea towel from the rack beside the sink and wrapped it carefully round her left hand with a gentleness she would never have believed him capable of.

'Where do you keep the rest of them?' he asked brusquely, and Tarin indicated with a nod of her head, the drawer where the clean tea towels were kept.

She was willing enough to let him take charge for the moment because she was too shocked to speak and her fingers were throbbing painfully, although the left one was already slightly less fierce and burning wrapped in the cool softness of the cloth. He took another tea towel from the drawer and wrapped it just as efficiently round her right hand, then reached round her to untie the apron strings.

The rather threadbare cotton ties tangled briefly and she was momentarily enveloped in a strong, spicy masculine warmth as he reached round her with both hands. Her face was close to the broad smoothness of his chest where the pale blue shirt opened and she felt her knees become so weak that she felt sure she must fall if he didn't soon move away. Managing to free the apron ties at last, he pulled the apron over her head and flung it down on to a chair.

'I'm taking you down to Doctor Robertson,' he informed her without consultation, and led her to the door, unprotesting, until she realised what he had said.

'No! No, there's no need!' she denied, pulling back against the hand that held her arm in a grip she could not hope to break. 'I'm all right, I don't need a doctor!'

He took not the slightest notice of her objections, as she might have guessed, but led her, still protesting, down the garden path to where his car was parked on the narrow winding road that led down to the village. It was a large, black, expensive-looking monster that the whole village was bound to recognise, and she could just imagine the gossip it would arouse if she was seen driving with him, even if it was only as far as Doctor Robertson's house on the far side of the village.

He opened the passenger door and tucked her into the seat, carefully arranging her skirt over her knees before he slammed the door, and seemed quite unconcerned about what anyone thought, which, of course, was typical of him.

'I really don't need to bother the doctor with this,' she insisted as he slid into the seat beside her, and he looked at her for a second down the length of his arrogant nose, his mouth showing that hint of a sternness again as he started the engine.

'Don't be heroic, Tarin,' he told her coolly.

'I'm not,' she objected. 'I just don't want to make a fuss, that's all.'

He sent the big car purring along the narrow road at a speed that was quite unnecessary in the circumstances, and spared a brief glance at her slightly bewildered face. 'You've burnt your fingers quite badly,' he told her with the air of explaining elementary points to a rather slow child. 'I can't have you laid up with your hands too badly hurt for work for goodness knows how long!'

Almost in tears from the pain in her hands, Tarin felt the first betraying drop tremble on her lashes when she heard his severely practical reasons for concern. 'Oh, I see,' she said in a small choked voice. 'You're worried about me not being able to work—I wondered why you were so concerned about me! I should have known, of course!'

'Don't you *want* to have them healed as soon as possible?' he asked reasonably, not yet noticing the tears, and Tarin nodded.

'Yes, of course I do, but——' She bit her lip, trying to do something about the tears that now ran down her face quite freely, using the tea towels that bound her hands to brush them away as best she could. 'Oh, it doesn't matter!'

'You're crying!'

He sounded so surprised that she wondered if he imagined her some kind of curious creature who did the unexpected. It was surely enough to make any girl cry, first burning her hands painfully and then having her boss tell her that he wanted her to get well as soon as possible simply because he needed her to work for him.

'What do you expect?' she asked huskily, the tears still running down her cheeks. 'My hands hurt and you—you're not exactly sympathetic, are you?'

'Oh dear!' She couldn't see his expression very clearly for the tears in her eyes, but she thought he looked as if he was smiling, and that made her angry.

'You *are* a self-centred, unfeeling creature!' she accused recklessly. 'You just don't care about my feelings at all, do you?'

He said nothing for a moment, but drove the car in through a pair of slightly weather-worn iron gates that guarded Doctor Robertson's untidy front garden. Turning in his seat after he stopped the car, he looked at her tear-stained face for a moment in silence, then swiftly, and quite unexpectedly, he leaned across and kissed her cheek lightly. His nearness brought again that spicy warm maleness that had enveloped her at the house when he untied her apron, and she stared at him for a moment, with her lips parted in surprise.

'It's too late to do much about it now,' he said quietly, as he leaned further across and opened the door for her, 'but I'll see what I can do about impressing you with my sympathy after the doctor's seen you.'

Doctor Robertson was a kind, elderly man, and Tarin remembered that he had once treated her for measles when she was quite small and staying with her uncle and aunt during the school holidays. He remembered her too, and clucked and frowned over her hands for several minutes.

'It could have been much worse,' he decreed at last. 'You were lucky, my dear girl. But you must not use your hands for a day or two.'

Tarin looked not very pleased about that, but she had expected something of the sort so she could not pretend to be surprised by it. 'That's going to be difficult,' she said while the doctor applied acqua-flavin to her fingertips. 'But I suppose there's nothing for it.'

He saw her out and exchanged a few words with Darrel, then reminded her again about not using her hands. 'Oh, I have the week-end for them to heal,' she told him, and glanced at Darrel. 'I have to be ready for work on Monday morning.'

She heard his huff of impatience as she said it and he took her arm with a curiously disturbing air of possessiveness. 'You'll do no such thing,' he told her shortly. 'And stop trying to make me appear as some kind of inhuman monster, for heaven's sake!'

Doctor Robertson raised one grey eyebrow and appeared to find their exchange of some interest, but Tarin was not prepared to let the present situation become the source of village gossip. The old doctor was known to be a notorious old gossip and she could see that he already had quite the wrong idea about her relationship with Darrel Bruce, an idea no doubt fostered by that possessive hand on her arm as he guided her across the surgery to the door.

'I'm sorry if I gave that impression,' she told him, then smiled at the old man again gratefully. 'Thank you for seeing me out of surgery hours, Doctor Robertson,' she told him. 'I won't use my hands any more than I can help, but it's a bit difficult when I have to cook for myself and my uncle.'

Doctor Robertson looked at her from beneath his bushy brows and smiled. 'Robert McCourt's managed to survive on his own cooking for the past few years,' he said. 'He can manage again, I dare say!'

'I suppose so.' She sounded so unsure that the old doctor patted her arm consolingly.

'Never you mind, lassie,' he said kindly, 'you'll

soon heal. You're a healthy young girl and you'll soon be working away as good as new in a wee while.'

He followed them out to the car and as they walked down the steps Tarin endeavoured to shake off that embarrassingly possessive hand on her arm. 'I could walk back quite easily,' she told Darrel, but he shook his head.

'You could, he said bluntly, 'but I'm seeing your uncle, remember?'

'You're visiting Robert McCourt?' the doctor asked with deceptive mildness, and Tarin knew as well as anyone how unlikely that would sound to a local who knew all about the feud that had never ended as far as the McCourts were concerned.

Darrel smiled a little ruefully, knowing how that would be circulated round the village, with interest. 'I have some business I want to discuss with him,' he said. 'That's how I came to be on hand when Tarin hurt herself.'

His use of her christian name seemed to have become firmly established, she noticed, and was rather pleased about it, although whether her uncle would feel as pleased was another matter.

'It's a good job you were there,' the doctor ventured softly. 'A young woman needs a man's help at times like this, no matter how independent she may be, eh, Miss McCourt?'

Tarin merely smiled, saying nothing that would either confirm or deny his theory, and Darrel's fingers tightened momentarily on her arm, as if he approved of her silence. The doctor watched while Darrel saw her into the car again, and nodded his head, evidently finding confirmation in the act of courtesy.

'It's a grand thing when such nonsense as a feud ends,' he said in his soft voice, still apparently trying to see what he wanted to see in their behaviour. 'It's high time, you'll agree!'

Neither of his callers answered, but for a brief moment Tarin looked into Darrel's brown eyes and saw the deep glint of laughter that enjoyed the old man's persistence. 'Feeling O.K.?' he asked softly, and she nodded.

Driving back through the village neither of them said a word, but the one time that Tarin ventured a glance at him from the concealment of her lashes she met his gaze full on her and hastily looked away again. The glitter of laughter was still there and she found it infinitely disturbing.

'I don't know why you find my being hurt so funny,' she told him, her mouth unconsciously pouting reproach.

'I don't!' His denial was only to be expected, of course.

'Then why——' she began, and he laughed softly.

'I'm thinking what old Doc Robertson's going to make of this little caper,' he said.

'And you find *that* funny?'

Her blue eyes sparkled indignantly, and she foresaw, all too easily, another quarrel looming. Public opinion, she thought, had never deterred the Bruces, and the present holder of the name was no exception. It wouldn't worry him that Doctor Robertson would probably be regaling his cronies with whatever interpretation he had put on their visit. Her own prickly, uneasy manner and that possessive hand on her arm, the warmth in those brown eyes when he looked at her—there was so much that could be misinterpreted and she, for one, was not happy about it; her uncle would be even less so.

'You're afraid for your reputation?' he suggested softly, and Tarin did not answer. 'Or are you afraid of what your uncle might say when he hears you've been seen with the Bruce?'

'Please don't laugh about Uncle Robert,' she begged in a husky little voice. 'He—he's very serious about it, you know.'

'I know,' he said quietly. 'But sooner or later he's going to have to see the light, isn't he, Tarin?' The brown eyes glanced at her briefly again over his shoulder. 'If you really want to see an end to this ancient nonsense,' he pointed out, 'your uncle won't have much choice.'

'I do,' Tarin assured him without hesitation. 'You know I do!'

'I *hope* you do,' he corrected her softly, and pulled up outside her uncle's house, turning in his seat for a minute to look at her steadily. 'And *if* you do you're going to have to work at it, Tarin.'

'I—I know.'

Her heart was beating so hard she could scarcely hear what he was saying, and she licked her lips in her nervousness. So much, it seemed, depended on her, and on Darrel too, although she suspected she would be expected to make most of the effort.

One large hand reached out and enclosed hers in strong brown fingers that curled tightly for a moment encouragingly. 'We'll make it,' he said confidently.

Robert McCourt arrived home only minutes after Tarin came back with Darrel, and she guessed he would be more than simply curious to see Darrel's car outside, if indeed he recognised it. In fact he looked quite stunned when he found him actually in his house, and for a moment Tarin held her breath in case he ordered him out.

Common sense and good manners prevailed, however, and he merely murmured a polite greeting, as if to a stranger, and asked what he could do for him. It was then that he noticed there was something wrong with her hands and he frowned anxiously.

'Tarin!' he said, taking her hands in his and staring at the red and angry tips covered with acqua-flavin. 'What on earth have you done, lassie?'

'It's a long story,' Tarin told him ruefully. 'But I'm all right, Robert, honestly. I burnt my hands taking a hot cake tin out of the oven, but fortunately Mr. Bruce was here and he ran me down to see Doctor Robertson. It's nothing to worry about.'

Assured of her recovery, her uncle immediately took up the fact of Darrel Bruce having been visiting his home while he was absent, and he frowned at him curiously. 'You were here?' he asked bluntly, and Darrel half smiled.

He could guess, Tarin thought, what it cost her uncle to have a member of the family he still thought of as enemies, actually under his roof, and probably visiting his niece in his absence. Probably it amused Darrel, but it would certainly not amuse her uncle and she was anxious to let him know the reason for the visit without delay.

'Mr. Bruce has some business he wants to discuss with you, Robert,' she told him. 'I think I'll go and see what I can do about that mess in the kitchen while you talk to him.'

'Business?' Her uncle's frown was even more puzzled, and he looked at Darrel watching Tarin leave the room.

'Take it easy with those hands,' Darrel warned, and she turned and looked at him over her shoulder, a strangely lilting sensation in the region of her heart as she met his eyes which were grave but glowing dark.

'I'll be careful,' she promised softly, and closed the sitting-room door behind her.

CHAPTER FIVE

SOMETHING Tarin had always enjoyed, even as a child, was walking, especially in such country as this, and since she was unable to do anything much with her hands for the time being, she took advantage of her enforced idleness and went for a long walk the following day. Her uncle had assured her that he could cope quite adequately with what cooking there was to do, so she had taken herself off with an easy conscience.

The events of yesterday had given her much food for thought and she wondered if she was being too optimistic in thinking that the much desired end to the feud was even nearer than she dared hope. Darrel had seemed so serious about them working for that end together and she saw no reason to doubt his sincerity.

It had been something of a minor triumph to learn that her uncle had agreed to supply Deepwater with some badly needed pumps for the hotel's private water supply, and she guessed that Darrel had made a better impression on Robert that he was prepared to admit.

As old Doctor Robertson had said, the whole silly business had gone on for far too long, and if the present generation could be the means of ending it once and for all, then so much the better. Darrel and her uncle had apparently come to some agreement, and although her uncle had said little about it to her afterwards, despite his reticence she sensed he was quite pleased to have the hotel's custom. His was quite a small business despite the fact that it was doing very well.

With her surroundings lending themselves to undistracted thought, she dwelt on one subject after another, going over in her mind all that had happened since her return to Deepwater. Finding Darrel so different from the youth she remembered with such clarity had been somewhat upsetting, but his older image had been even more disturbing. For all that she had moments of misgiving she had not had any real cause to regret her move north.

She enjoyed her work most of the time, and she was forced to admit that she had worked for worse employers than Darrel. She got along well with Mrs. Smith—her defensive rudeness to Darrel had soon been forgotten, and she seldom saw the rest of the staff.

She'd come into contact with few of the guests, except the American, Conrad Stein, and she spent a moment wondering if he had left the hotel altogether, for she had seen nothing more of him since that first meeting on the carriageway. He had expressed a wish at the time to see her again, but probably that had been no more than a somewhat flattering form of politeness.

Whatever it was, she had not seen him since, and she shrugged him out of her thoughts and gave her mind to other things as she continued with her solitary walk. No one could be out of temper for very long in such surroundings, she felt sure.

She was enjoying the warmth of the sun and the cool fresh breeze that kept it from being too hot. The hills, even those close at hand, had a misty, ethereal look that she always found so enchanting, and the same soft, dreamy atmosphere enhanced Stonebeck—as if that mysterious village of legend might appear at any minute in its green hollow, ribboned with silver water.

The soft cushion of budding heather gave a spring to her step as she walked, heading for the tiny loch of Torin's Pool that sat like a gem in its beautiful setting. The water was still, but for a faint, almost indiscernible ripple across its surface, stirred by the light wind, and it mirrored a clear blue sky fluffed over with white clouds.

The little loch always looked so incredibly deep, despite its small surface area, and she had heard legends of it being haunted by a past McCourt who had drowned in its peaty depths. Perhaps, she pondered wryly, driven to desperation by a contempory Bruce.

A windblown rowan hung its head near the water's edge as a reminder of bleaker days and several beeches huddled into a mass of pale spring green along its banks, while the last catkins still danced on the branches of the sauch or goat willow.

The only sounds to be heard were the whisper of the wind stirring the trees and the distant throaty cry of a pheasant somewhere. The whole scene had a tranquillity that Tarin found just as moving as its beauty, and she stood for some time at the water's edge with her eyes closed and her face lifted to the cooling wind.

It was some instinct, some sense that she was no longer alone, that made her open her eyes suddenly and turn her head, and she frowned. No specific sound had warned her of anyone approaching, for even a horse's hooves were deadened by the cushioning heather, but when she looked over her shoulder the only moving thing was a horseman coming her way. It was only now, as he came nearer, that she heard the first faint steely jingle of harness.

Seeing the rider her first thought had been that it must be Darrel, but a second look assured her it wasn't. The figure was shorter and thinner and less, just a little less, expert, if she could count herself any judge. Whether he too recognised her, she was unsure, but certainly he urged his horse to greater speed and came racing towards her, and she recognised Conrad Stein.

Her reaction to his appearance was somewhat mixed, for although she had liked him well enough at their first meeting some weeks before, she was reluctant to have such peace as Stonebeck offered disturbed by a stranger, no matter how charming. Whether she wanted his company or not, however, it was plain that he meant to join her and she could see that he was smiling as he came.

She had to admit that he was an excellent rider, but he lacked Darrel's style and panache, his air of arrogant self-confidence, and consequently he appeared less impressive. Despite her reluctance to have her peace invaded she nevertheless gave him a smile of recognition as he joined her.

He reined in his mount and dismounted almost in one movement and stood beside her, his smile wider than ever, as if he had no doubt at all that he would be welcome. 'Hello, Miss McCourt!'

'Mr. Stein.'

Before she had time to even remember her hands he had grasped them firmly in greeting and she winced, despite an effort not to. He looked at her anxiously, startled by her reaction. 'Gee, I'm sorry,' he said hastily. 'Did I hurt you?'

Smiling ruefully, Tarin nursed her two hands together against her chest. 'It wasn't your fault, Mr. Stein,' she told him. 'I had an accident yesterday and my hands are a bit painful.'

'An accident?' He looked even more anxious. 'Not too serious, I hope.'

'It was entirely my own fault,' she admitted readily. 'I should have known better than to take a hot tin from the oven without a cloth.'

'They're burnt?' He took both her hands this time and bent over them anxiously for a moment. 'I am sorry, I hope I didn't hurt you too much— they look kind of sore.'

'They are,' she said with a rueful smile. 'But I've no one to blame but myself.'

She was quite glad in a way, now that he was there, that he had joined her, and she smiled at him encouragingly while he retained his hold on her hands, the reins draped on one arm. It was obvious from the expression on his boyish-looking face that his pleasure at seeing her again was quite genuine, and she could not possibly object to that.

'I somehow never expected to see you again,' he said. 'Do you always come out here and walk alone, like this?'

'Quite often,' Tarin told him, wondering if she was misreading the intention in his eyes. 'More especially when the weather's as nice as it is now. I love this late spring, early summer weather, don't you? And the scenery is absolutely breathtaking, don't you think so?'

'Quite beautiful!'

The expression in his voice and the look in his eyes made it plain that he applied the adjective as much to her personally as to either the weather or the surrounding scenery, and the realisation gave her a warm glow of well-being suddenly.

A man like Conrad Stein was just what she needed for her morale when Darrel Bruce was in one of his autocratic moods. Someone to soothe and console her, and it was a pity, she mused ruefully, that she had not had the benefit of the American's morale-boosting company only a couple of days ago when she had suffered a badly bruised ego.

A quite minor point of office business had caused one of their inevitable differences and, as usual, she had come off worst in the exchange. Darrel had verbally beaten her and she would have welcomed someone like Conrad Stein to help make her forget the experience. Conrad Stein, she felt quite sure in her own mind, would never, as Darrel had done, tell his secretary that she could either do as she was damned well told or get out.

She hadn't taken him at his word, of course, and he had been very kind and helpful yesterday, when she had hurt her hands, even if his kindness was suspect. It did a lot to make up for his bad temper the day before, although it was not the first time they had clashed violently and she doubted if it would be the last.

Both she and Darrel had pretty forceful tempers, and he was inclined to be impatient with her more conventional methods of doing things, so they were bound to clash on a number of points. Having someone like Conrad Stein to turn to in moments of crisis could well be the antidote she needed, if he was as anxious to further their acquaintance as he appeared to be.

Remembering how he had stated a wish to see

her again at their first meeting, she was puzzled by his not having done so. 'I wondered why you——' She shook her head and hesitated to go on, then looked at him from the shadow of her long lashes and again wondered if there was a good reason for his not having contacted her. 'I wondered if you'd remembered me,' she said, and he immediately reached for her hand again, stroking her fingers as if to impress her with the truth of what he was saying.

'I've been away for a while,' he told her, 'and then when I tried to come in and see you after I got back your boss put up the bar!'

Tarin blinked at him a little dazedly for a moment. 'Did he?' she said huskily.

It was something of a surprise to think of him standing guard to make sure that no one came and interrupted her while she was working. It was surprising too that Conrad Stein had not laid down the law more insistently—after all, he was a paying guest as far as she knew, and surely entitled to a certain amount of concession.

'He said you were busy,' he explained. 'And he'd rather I didn't bother you while you were working, and—well, you know how Darrel can be! He'd as soon have kicked me out if I'd gone against him!'

Tarin looked at him curiously, smiling at the seriousness of the statement. 'Oh, surely not, Mr. Stein,' she said. 'You *are* a guest at the hotel, after all.'

'Not quite in the usual sense,' he denied, but didn't make any other explanation, so that Tarin was more puzzled than ever about just what he and his sister were doing there, unless they were private guests. Certainly from the way Gloria Stein walked around in and out of the office, it looked that way. 'Anyway——' he shrugged and pulled a face, 'I just lay low and hoped I'd spot you off duty some time.'

'And you have,' Tarin smiled.

'Sure, the luck of the Steins!'

Evidently, Tarin thought, she had been right to assume that Darrel would not like his staff mixing with the guests, whether paying or private, and for a moment she tried to see snobbery as one of his faults and couldn't. But there could surely be no other reason for his refusing to let Conrad Stein come in and see her.

'I spotted you from way back!' he grinned, and his youthful-looking face appeared more school-boyish than ever. 'Don't tell me that prayers are never answered!'

'I'm sorry you had so much trouble trying to see me,' she said with a smile. 'But as you say, I do know how Mr. Bruce can be.'

'Isn't he the limit?' Conrad asked, shaking his head. 'You'd think he owns you, not simply pays you to work for him, the way he lays down the law! Don't you ever feel like kicking up?'

'Sometimes!' Tarin laughed, wondering again at his frankness with a virtual stranger.

'But you never do?' he asked, and she pulled a wry face.

'Quite often,' she told him ruefully, 'but it doesn't do me much good, I'm afraid! I've never won an argument yet!'

'Does he bully you?'

They were walking together along the side of the tiny loch as they talked, with Conrad Stein leading his horse, and adapting his normally longer stride to suit her more leisurely pace. Being still unsure just what his standing was with Darrel, she hesitated to be too frank with him, even though she had said nothing so far that wasn't completely true.

'Oh, I'm used to all kinds,' she told him with a laugh. 'A secretary has to be.'

'I guess so.'

They walked in silence for a while, side by side, with the warm summer silence enveloping them and the soft wind stirring Tarin's dark hair and cooling her forehead. She always thought of Stonebeck as a kind of miniature Paradise, and wondered if Conrad Stein shared her enthusiasm for it.

It was some time before either of them spoke again, and Tarin did so then only because she could see another rider coming their way and recognised him, even at a distance. It could only be Darrel who rode like that, coming at such breakneck speed through the springy heather on the same big brown stallion he always rode. The animal's strength stretched to its limit, tail and mane streaming in the light wind.

'I think we're about to have company,' she said quietly, and tried desperately to do something about the rapid hammering of her heartbeat as she watched him come.

There was something almost savagely beautiful about the whole scene. The man and the flying horse and the softly beautiful hills and glens as a background for their furious haste, and she felt her senses respond to it ugently. It was at once both frightening and blood-stirringly exciting to witness the skill of the rider and the superb sure-footedness of his mount, especially when she knew that one moment of doubt could send them both hurtling down to serious injury or worse.

'Just look at him go!'

The half-whispered admiration was involuntary, Tarin thought, for the expression on Conrad Stein's face was not as friendly as she would have expected. In fact he looked as if Darrel Bruce was the last person he wanted to see at that moment.

Such an exhibition would have been showing off if anyone else had had the nerve to do it, Tarin mused ruefully, but Darrel would scorn the need to do anything so childish. He rode like that because he enjoyed the challenge and the sense of power it gave him, she felt sure. He would actually enjoy risking his neck by riding at that furious pace just for the sheer thrill of it.

He came straight for them and she saw a faint frown on her companion's face when she spared him a glance. 'What's he done with Gloria?' Con said half under his breath, and Tarin pointed to the distance, some hundred yards or more behind Darrel's speeding figure, to another rider, coming less recklessly fast.

She needed no one to tell her that the figure crouched over the horse's neck was Gloria Stein, and her laughter was instinctive as she watched the American girl trying to catch up with Darrel. It reminded her of the old days when as a schoolgirl she had worshipped him from afar and seen him so many times outpace a younger Gloria Stein with his horsemanship.

'She never could catch up with him!' she declared with such obvious relish that Conrad Stein turned and looked at her curiously for a moment.

'Couldn't she?' he asked quietly, too quietly, and Tarin realised at last what she had said and how tactless she had been in the circumstances.

'I remember when I was here as a child,' she told him, trying to make some sort of explanation. 'I used to see Darrel—Mr. Bruce, riding then, and your sister was often trying to keep up with him, but I don't think I ever saw her do so. He rides too fast!'

'He's good,' he said quietly and rather grudgingly, and Tarin wondered yet again why he sounded so much as if he disliked his host. She hadn't seen him as so unfriendly towards him the last time they met.

It was only moments later that horse and rider joined them at the lochside. The brown stallion was reined in hard, tossing his head and breathing deeply like some mythical creature, with vapour issuing in jets from his flared nostrils, and the ripple of muscle in Darrel's long legs left no doubt as to who was in command.

'Hello, Tarin.'

Both the quiet voice and the steady brown eyes excluded her companion from the initial greeting, and Tarin knew without doubt that Conrad Stein resented it, as he resented the intrusion of someone else into their quiet walk.

'Hello, Mr. Bruce.' Tarin's reply was brief and she sought for reasons why she should feel so nervous and uneasy just because he had found her in the company of the American.

'How are your hands?' he asked, then gave her no chance to reply before he interrupted with another question. 'You haven't been using them, have you?'

Tarin shook her head. 'No, of course I haven't!'

'There's no of course about it,' Darrel retorted. 'If you felt like using them then you would, no matter how foolhardy it was! I know you!'

She gave him a swift, scornful look from under her lashes and stuck out her chin as she answered. 'Not as well as you think you do, obviously!' she replied shortly, and was not really surprised to see him smile.

'Obviously!' he echoed softly, and at last spared her companion a glance. 'I wondered where you'd got to, Con,' he told him. 'Couldn't you keep up?'

Conrad Stein's resentment, both of Darrel's arrival and his manner, showed plainly in the slightly sulky expression he wore. 'I wasn't trying to keep up,' he told him in a rather hard, flat voice, and the hand holding the reins showed bone white at the knuckles. 'I had ideas of my own.'

'So I see.' Darrel again looked at Tarin, and it was evident from the way his brown eyes watched her, narrowed and faintly curious, that he was uncertain just what he had interrupted. 'I hope I didn't interrupt a—rendezvous,' he said quietly, and Tarin's first instinct was to deny it hastily, but she had no opportunity.

'Now you know you did,' Conrad Stein said in that same flat voice, 'why not get yourself lost again?' The grey eyes had a bright challenging look that made Tarin uneasy. 'You can't still keep guard on your secretary, you know,' he went on with obvious relish and gaining confidence from the fact that so far Darrel had made no attempt to interrupt him. 'This isn't your office, Darrel, out here Tarin's a free agent.'

She rather dazedly noted the familiar use of her christian name and wondered if she should do something to correct the impression he was bound to give if he went on in the same vein. Darrel was still watching her and it gave her a curiously vulnerable feeling to have him scrutinising her so closely, almost as if he suspected she did not share her companion's dislike of his appearance on the scene.

'Tarin's always a free agent, as far as I'm concerned,' he said quietly. 'Have I ever suggested otherwise, Tarin?'

'Not to me.' She looked up at last and saw the glint of surprise her answer caused, and the raised brow.

'Who else?' he asked softly, and she hastily and quite inadvertently glanced at Conrad Stein before shaking her head.

She remembered that Conrad Stein could prove a useful boost to her self-confidence the next time Darrel got the better of her, and she hesitated to betray the fact that he had said as much as he had to her, so she shook her head and said nothing, leaving him to guess what confidences they had exchanged before his arrival.

'I see!' he said shortly, obviously needing no verbal confirmation of the betraying glance. 'I'm sorry I interrupted!'

Tarin made great play of being offhand and shrugged carelessly.

'It doesn't matter,' she told him casually.

He regarded her for a moment longer with curiosity and she saw the way his lip curled slightly, as if he either saw through her pretence, or despised her for meeting his wealthy American guest on the sly. He looked as disturbing as ever he did, up there on that great, fire-breathing animal, and she despaired of her self-control when her heart pounded so heavily in her breast as she looked up at him briefly.

Cream trousers hugged those long legs today and a pale blue shirt showed off the deep mahogany tan to advantage, the open neck revealing the strong column of throat and neck and, below, the first broad smoothness of his chest. Short sleeves bared his arms to the sun and his broad brown hands lay eased slightly on the reins now that his mount was resting after that furious gallop.

'Aren't you with Gloria?' Conrad asked pointedly, as if he was unaware of his sister riding furiously in their direction, and Darrel's smile showed that he recognised his motives.

'She's coming,' he said quietly. 'I wanted to go flat out and her Bunty isn't up to Tarquin's standard.'

Instinctively Tarin turned and looked across to where Gloria Stein came swiftly across the heathery turf towards them. It would be nice to be able to ride so that she could come flying across the moorland too, but an expressed wish to learn now would almost certainly be misinterpreted, at least by one of them.

'Do you ride, Miss McCourt?' Conrad asked, reverting to the formality of her title, but possibly foreseeing the chance of further meetings if she rode.

The possibilities open to her were endless, Tarin could see that, and it appealed to her immensely at the moment. She could not only ride with Conrad Stein, but perhaps, when she was good enough and he had the patience, she could accompany Darrel. Scarcely giving the thought time to dwell in her mind, she dismissed the latter part as highly unlikely.

But still it was possible that she could learn and

it would open up the countryside to her. She was aware suddenly that she had not yet answered his question and she shook her head hastily. 'I never learned,' she confessed.

'Oh, but you should,' Conrad insisted earnestly. 'You'd love it.'

She was aware that both Darrel and Conrad were watching her with definite interest and her heart was banging away at her ribs as she thought over the possibilities. 'Living all my life in a town,' she explained, 'I've never had much opportunity to learn.'

'Do you want to learn?'

She was not really aware of watching Darrel as she replied, but briefly she met the curiously glittering look in the brown eyes and it stirred her pulses into the inevitable response. 'I—I'd like to——'

'I'll teach you!'

The words left Darrel's lips only a fraction of a second before Conrad said, 'If you'd like to learn, I'll willingly teach you,' and there followed a long, uneasy silence while Tarin sought for words to fill it—and failed.

It was typical of Darrel, of course, to make his offer a statement and not merely a suggestion, as Conrad had done. It would not even occur to him that she would refuse, and there was a hint of laughter in the brown eyes when he looked down at her, his wide mouth just tilted at one corner.

'Offers from all sides,' he mocked softly. 'It seems you have a choice, Tarin.'

It was an embarrassing position to be in and Tarin suspected he realised it well enough and found it amusing. Conrad Stein, on the other hand, looked faintly sulky, as if he lacked Darrel's confidence and was quite sure which of them she would choose to let teach her.

The temptation to turn to Darrel was almost irresistible, but she resisted it firmly, prompted by the certainty that he would be a hard taskmaster in that as in everything else, and she would hate to have him scorn her beginner's efforts. It was the thought of looking a complete fool while she was learning that finally decided her as he sat up there looking down at her with that hint of a smile still on his face and a glitter of challenge in his eyes.

'Well, Tarin?' he said softly, and she spared him a long, uncertain look before she turned and smiled at Conrad Stein.

'I'd love to learn if you have the time, Mr. Stein,' she said in a small husky voice.

She dared not look at Darrel again, but she sensed the way he drew himself up sharply, refusing to try and persuade her to change her mind and angry because for once he had been very pointedly turned down. Almost before the words were out of her mouth she regretted her choice, but it was too late now. Darrel was angry with her for snubbing him and Conrad was so pleased that his smile was wide and triumphant as he looked up at his host.

'Sure, I have the time,' he told her. 'You say when, and I'll be there!'

'I'll—I'll have to think about it first.' The idea was less attractive now that it was more or less fact, and she was all too aware of Gloria Stein bearing down on them, her blonde hair dishevelled and her blue eyes hard and angry.

'One of these days,' she said as she came up to them, and addressing herself to Darrel, 'I'll catch you up, you black-hearted Highlander, I swear it!'

He turned a broad but wry smile on her, and shook his head. 'You won't,' he informed her with certainty. 'Tarquin's uncatchable!'

'Like you!'

The retort was swift and bitter, and Tarin felt sure that Gloria Stein immediately regretted having made it. Darrel briefly cocked one dark brow at her, then sought and held Tarin's reluctant gaze as he spoke. 'Don't be too sure,' he said softly, and for some inexplicable reason Tarin hastily bit her lip and looked away.

CHAPTER SIX

IT was another couple of days before Tarin's hands were well enough for her to consider going back to work, and she viewed the prospect with mixed feelings. Darrel was unlikely to care one way or the other whether he taught her to ride, or whether Conrad Stein did, but what he would inevitably resent was her making her choice so baldly obvious in front of the other man.

She arrived at Deepwater on the following Wednesday morning feeling quite incredibly nervous. It had been not only rash but also unforgivably rude of her to snub him so pointedly in favour of his American guest and she wondered what kind of a reception she could expect.

Sighing deeply, she climbed the worn steps to the front doors and let herself in—there was nothing for it but to face the music. As on her first morning, there was no one around in the big hall as she made her way across to the office, and her heels clicked loudly on the stone-flagged floor.

The gaze of Darrel's fierce, red-haired ancestors followed her relentlessly and gave her no cause to suppose that the current upholder of the family honour would deal with her any less ruthlessly than they would have done themselves. Perhaps she could suggest that fear of offending a guest had prompted her to act the way she had—only she wasn't sure she had the nerve to suggest it.

She was just about to open the office door when a voice called out to her from the other side of the hall, and she turned swiftly, startled out of her reverie. 'Miss McCourt!' Conrad Stein came hurrying towards her, his boyish face beaming a smile. 'It's good to see you again,' he told her. 'How're your hands?'

Tarin extended them, palms upwards, showing the pink and shiny fingertips. 'Quite well now, Mr. Stein, thank you.'

'Good!' He took her hands in his and bent to look at them more closely, then pulled a sympathetic face. 'Say, that must have hurt!'

'It did,' she agreed, and as unobtrusively as possible drew her hands from his. 'But it was my own fault, so I can't complain too loudly.'

'And are they healed enough to hold the reins?' he asked, and for a second Tarin frowned at him curiously, 'You said I could be your riding instructor,' he reminded her, and she smiled warily.

'Oh yes! Yes, I'd forgotten.'

The rather earnest grey eyes noted her lack of enthusiasm and looked at her questioningly. 'You haven't changed your mind, have you?' he asked.

Tarin chose not to look at him while she answered. It had seemed easy enough to make the sudden decision to learn to ride while she was out there in the peace of Stonebeck and she could see no pitfalls, but she had since had cause to regret even mentioning it.

Conrad Stein, she guessed, would not easily relinquish the idea, but she must somehow try and convince him that there were good reasons for her having second thoughts. If only she had not told him that her hands were well again she could have used that as an excuse, now he would surely see through it.

'I—I haven't exactly changed my mind,' she told him at last, and he eyed her with vague suspicion.

'You haven't decided to accept Darrel's offer after all?' he suggested, and she hastily shook her head, glancing behind her at the closed door of the office.

'Oh no, of course not,' she told him. 'But there are a few snags, you know.'

'Like?'

'Well, for one thing I haven't the proper clothes,' she ventured, and he looked down at her neat, navy linen dress, then shook his head.

'All you need is a pair of denim pants and a shirt,' he told her. 'Do you have those?'

She nodded. 'But I still don't have the most important thing of all.'

'The horse?' he guessed with a faint smile. 'There's no problem there. There are plenty of horses in the stables here.'

'Oh, but I couldn't take one of those!' she objected hastily. 'They're for the use of the hotel guests, Mr. Stein, and I'm quite sure Mr. Bruce wouldn't like one of his staff members simply helping herself when she felt like it.'

'But why should he mind?' Conrad asked, reasonably enough he seemed to think, and it occurred to Tarin to wonder just how well he really knew his host. 'Holy smoke!' he went on, warming to his subject, 'this isn't the Middle Ages! That master-servant stuff went out with slavery, honey! You're as good as anyone else around here and I don't see why you can't ride one of the horses!'

'But I can't,' she insisted. 'At least not without asking Mr. Bruce first, and I can't see——'

'O.K., then we'll ask him!'

It promised to be so easy the way he said it, but Tarin knew well enough it wouldn't be anything of the sort and she certainly had no intention of asking Darrel herself for permission. Not after her deliberate snub of him, he would only dismiss her request out of hand and probably tell her exactly what he thought of her nerve into the bargain.

She looked at him warily. 'You—you don't expect me to ask him, do you?' she asked, and he shrugged.

'Well, you'd be the best person, honey,' he assured her. 'You're a beautiful girl and no man likes saying no to a beautiful girl, least of all Darrel Bruce!'

'Oh, but I——' She shook her head and looked at him for a moment through the thickness of her lashes, unwilling to admit, even to herself, that she could not face being snubbed in the way Darrel was bound to snub her if she asked him. 'I—I'd much rather you asked him, Mr. Stein,' she said.

'O.K.' He looked at her for a moment with narrowed eyes that made him look far less boyish. 'Say, you really are scared of him, aren't you?'

'No! No, of course I'm not scared of him!' She was appalled to feel the warmth of colour in her cheeks and wondered what on earth he would make of that. 'It—it's just that——'

'O.K., O.K.,' he said with a grin. 'I'll ask him, on one condition.' Tarin looked at him curiously, and he shook his head. 'Nothing very serious,' he assured her. 'Just that you call me Con. I know you British think we kind of rush things on our side of the Atlantic, but I just love your pretty name, and if you use mine then I'll feel free to call you Tarin. O.K.?'

'Oh, yes, yes, of course!'

He seemed bent on making up for lost time, the time Darrel had denied him by barring him from the office, and Tarin saw no reason why she should object. He was charming and attractive and she saw no reason at all why she should not further their acquaintance.

His grin widened, almost as if he knew what was in her mind. 'Then what about coming round to the stables with me now and giving the horses the once over?' he suggested, but Tarin, one eye on the door behind her shook her head.

'Oh no, I couldn't,' she told him. 'Not now, I'm due in the office, Mr. Stein—I mean, Con.'

He too looked at the closed door and pulled a wry face. 'You think he's in already?' he asked, and she shrugged uneasily.

She felt rather like a conspirator talking about him half under her breath right outside the office door. 'It's quite possible,' she said, and glanced at her watch. 'And it is time I went in.'

'Not just for a couple of minutes?' he suggested persuasively.

'No, really——'

'Oh, come on, Tarin!' He smiled at her broadly and one hand under her elbow drew her away from the door and towards him. 'It won't take long.'

Knowing it was sheer folly to allow herself to be persuaded into anything so rash, Tarin held back, pulling her arm from his hold and shaking her head. 'No,' she insisted. 'I haven't the time now.'

'O.K.' He shrugged resignedly. 'Then we'll start you tomorrow.'

'Tomorrow?'

Her surprise made him frown briefly. 'Sure, why

not?' he asked.

There was no earthly reason why not, Tarin realised, except that no one had yet asked Darrel what he thought of her borrowing one of his horses. 'If you think Mr. Bruce *will* let me take one of his horses,' she said, 'then I suppose——'

Before she could finish the sentence she heard the office door open behind her and hastily bit her lip, cutting off the words. Darrel made no attempt to come out into the hall, but stood just inside the room with one hand on the door knob and his brown eyes taking swift appraisal of the situation. Then he cocked a brow at Tarin and looked rather pointedly at his wristwatch.

'I thought you weren't coming this morning after all,' he said, and instinctively she was on the defensive, looking at her own watch to check.

'I'm not late, Mr. Bruce,' she told him. 'At least no more than a couple of minutes.'

He ignored the argument and instead looked down at her hands. 'How are your hands?' he asked.

'Better, thank you.'

She did not extend them for inspection as she had in answer to Conrad's similar question, but curled her fingers into her palms. She felt not only nervous but quite unaccountably guilty at being caught talking to Conrad Stein in the hall, and yet there was no earthly reason why she should. It was no more than a couple of minutes past nine and he must realise that the delay was none of her doing.

Before she could take leave of her companion he reached out and took one of her hands, glancing at Darrel briefly before he spoke, half under his breath, as if he hoped he wouldn't be overheard.

'Don't forget tomorrow evening—I'll see you about seven by the stables,' he said, and squeezed her hand. 'So long for now, Tarin.'

'Goodbye, Con!'

An elevated brow commented on the familiarity of the first names, but Darrel said nothing for the moment, he merely stood back and held the door for her to come in. Then, when she was seated at her desk and ready to tackle the two days' correspondence that had accumulated during her absence, he came and sat on the edge of her desk, one booted foot swinging back and forth.

His proximity made Tarin nervous and she wondered if he was going to give her a lecture on the ethics of talking to his guests during working hours, instead he simply sat there and studied her silently for several moments while she sought to control her edgy nerves.

A dark navy crew-necked shirt and navy slacks gave him a rather darkly ominous air and she knew he was watching her while she took pad and pencil from her desk drawer. His scrutiny made her so nervous that eventually she dropped the pencil, and bit her lip in vexation at her own vulnerability.

Before she could stoop and retrieve the pencil he slid swiftly from the edge of the desk and retrieved it, then stood holding it in his hand while he resumed his scrutiny of her. 'Are you sure your hands are up to pounding a typewriter?' he asked, twirling the pencil between his own strong fingers, and Tarin nodded.

'Yes, I'm quite sure, thank you.'

'Show me!' The demand was brusque and he threw down the pencil and held out both his own hands.

After a brief hesitation Tarin obediently put her own hands into those broad, hard palms and felt her pulses respond to the touch of his strong fingers curling round her wrists. 'They're—they're fine,' she insisted huskily, but he looked doubtful.

'They look sore still,' he decided. 'You better take it easy today.'

Having no desire to be thought lacking in willingness to work she shook her head. 'I can manage,' she assured him. 'There must be an awful lot to do.'

'It'll keep!' He dismissed the accumulated mail with a shrug of his broad shoulders, and he still held her in that strong but gentle hold that affected her pulse rate so alarmingly. Then he raised her hands suddenly and for one heart-stopping second she thought he was going to kiss them. 'These,' he decided after examining her fingertips again, 'are not fit to hold reins. In case you don't realise it even the gentlest of horses makes a certain amount of pull on your hands.'

Tarin looked at him warily, then as hastily looked down again. 'I wasn't going to——' she began, but he shook his head and raised a querying brow.

'That was what you were plotting, out there, wasn't it?' he asked softly. 'The riding lessons you preferred to take from Con Stein?' She did not answer, but sat with her hands clasped uneasily in her lap. 'It had all the earmarks of a secret plot,' he went on relentlessly. 'Tell me, do you make a habit of meeting him out there at Stonebeck, like you did on Sunday?'

It was really nothing at all to do with him

whether or not she met Conrad Stein or how often, and she was tempted to tell him so, but the idea of his being interested enough to ask was intriguing and she did not answer for a moment. 'Not often,' she told him at last, evading the whole truth. 'But you don't like him trying to see me when I'm here, do you?'

'No.' His answer was blandly unconcerned whether it gave offence or not.

'Then there isn't much choice, is there?' she asked, and for some inexplicable reason found herself quite enjoying the situation.

'And that's why you chose to let him teach you to ride?'

His insistence was somehow uncharacteristic and she was more intrigued than ever as to the reason for it as she looked down at her shiny fingertips. 'In a way,' she allowed warily, and he gave a short, harsh laugh.

'In a way!' he mocked. 'Do you think I'm a complete idiot, Tarin?'

She looked up at him curiously, her heart tapping urgently at her ribs as she tried to find reasons for his apparent anger. 'You think I'm taking riding lessons, if I do, just so that I can see more of Mr. Stein?' she asked, and was surprised to notice how quiet and controlled she sounded.

'Aren't you?' he challenged, and she shook her head almost without thinking.

'No.' She looked down at her hands again. 'Anyway,' she said, 'I can't take riding lessons at all until I can afford to have my own horse, and that won't be for a very long time yet.'

He regarded her for a moment with his head tipped back slightly and one brow expressing doubt. 'From what I overheard just now, I thought you had that problem solved,' he said. 'Or was that all Con's idea?'

Tarin bit her lip wondering just how much he had heard through the door before he opened it and overheard her remark. Thinking to forestall the inevitable refusal she set her small chin at a firm angle and looked up with eyes that were much darker blue than usual, and dared him to think she was going to ask him about borrowing one of his horses.

'Mr. Stein had some idea about asking you to lend one of your horses,' she told him in a small, tight voice, prepared for a brusque refusal. 'But I told him I'd sooner not ask.'

'You did?' He sounded faintly surprised and his voice was quiet and incredibly soft, playing havoc with her senses, but she curled her hands tightly into themselves and refused to be touched by it. 'But why would you say that, Tarin?'

'Because I prefer to forget the whole thing rather than ask any favours!' she said, realising too late just how provocative it sounded.

'I see!'

There followed a long uncomfortable silence during which Tarin sat with her hands in her lap, regretting having been so impulsive. A glance at that strong face saw it set firmly against yielding an inch now that she had once again declared war, and she felt suddenly as if she wanted to cry. Quarrelling with him was the last thing she wanted and yet, as always she had made it inevitable and, as always, she regretted it bitterly.

His strong, square chin with its deep cleft, and the wide, stern mouth looked exactly like those fierce, red-haired old warriors out there in the hall, and they were enough to convince her that if the deadlock was to be broken, it would have to be through some move on her part. Sighing inwardly at the inevitability of it, she yielded to the inevitable.

'I don't expect you to lend me one of your horses,' she said in a small husky voice. 'You keep them for the use of your guests and I don't expect you to lend them to the people who work for you.'

His expression made his opinion of that quite obvious, and he looked at her down the length of his nose. 'Did Con Stein give you the idea that I was that much of a snob?' he asked. 'Or is it your own?'

He spoke quietly, although she sensed that being misjudged mattered quite a lot to him, and she suddenly felt rather small and mean. 'I—I just thought you might——' she began, and glanced up to find him shaking his head slowly.

'You really think that badly of me, Tarin?' he asked softly, and she shook her head silently. 'Then why imply it?' he pressed relentlessly, and again she shook her head without speaking.

For several seconds he stood looking at her, then he moved suddenly and came and perched himself once more on the edge of the desk. So close that she was enveloped in the warm vibrance of his masculinity and felt her pulses racing uncontrollably. When he swung one foot the taut, muscular tension of his thigh brushed against her and the open neck of his shirt, when he leaned forward to rest one forearm on his knee, gaped and gave a glimpse of reddish brown hair on the tanned breadth of his chest.

'What is it about me that keeps raising those McCourt prickles, Tarin?' he asked softly, and again she shook her head without answering. This time, however, he was not prepared to let her remain silent. He bent his head even lower and looked up into her face. 'Tarin?'

The gentle prompt was disturbing in itself and she bit her lip, looking down at the palms of her hands. 'I—I don't know that——'

The denial was cut short as she should have known it would be. 'Oh yes, you do,' he insisted, still in the same soft voice. 'Is it simply because of my name and you don't want to forget that out-dated old feud you pretend to despise? Do you want to keep it going after all, Tarin—is that it?'

She shook her head more firmly this time. 'No, no, of course I don't want to keep it going,' she denied. 'You know it isn't that.'

'Then why the prickles?' he insisted. 'Hmm?'

He reached out with one hand and touched her only lightly with a fingertip beside her left ear, but it was a sensual, shiver-inducing touch and she instinctively closed her eyes on the effect it had on her senses.

'Prickles aren't peculiar to the McCourts,' she told him in a small and rather shaky voice. 'You agreed that you're just as much to blame as I am— you know you are!'

His smile was brief and ironic and she half expected him to argue the point. 'Two hundred odd years have conditioned us to hate each other,' he said quietly, 'so I suppose no one can really blame us if we behave as if we do, can they?'

'Except that we're supposed to be the ones who are burying the hatchet,' Tarin reminded him with a resigned smile, and he nodded.

'Well, at least we're trying, aren't we?' he said quietly. 'If you—we stray occasionally who can blame us? At least we're making the effort!'

'On and off!'

Her attempt at lightness seemed to amuse him and he shook his head with a small, wry smile on his lips. 'We're not doing too badly,' he told her. 'Being the founders of a—a new age, I suppose you'd call it, isn't going to be easy, we shall have to work at it.' Tarin felt her heart fluttering wildly in her breast as she looked up at him, and again that evocative finger slid caressingly against her neck and set her pulses racing. 'A lot depends on us, doesn't it?' he asked softly.

'I—I suppose it does.' She felt strangely as if they were somewhere far distant from the rest of the world, and the subject of her borrowing one of the horses seemed to have been forgotten completely.

Someone, she thought dizzily, should do something about bringing them both back to earth, but she was strangely reluctant to do it. She realised how much her hands were trembling as she reached for the pencil he had discarded, and sat looking down at the blank pages of her notebook with unseeing eyes.

'You're very lovely.'

The deep, quiet voice slid along her spine like a shower of ice and she felt as if someone was depriving her of breath as she tried to control her chaotic emotions. That gentle, evocative caress stroked her neck until she could have cried out for it to stop if she was to keep her sanity.

'Darrel——' she was unaware of having used his christian name instead of the more formal title she usually gave him. 'Please——'

'Please?'

His eyes looked dark and glowing, but she was horribly unsure whether it was amusement for her almost childlike plea or some deeper emotion that made them glow like that. Then he leaned forward suddenly and the caressing hand curved to fit warmly round the smooth softness of her neck, drawing her towards him. His other hand reached out and curved about her waist, pulling her inexorably to her feet, and she noted vaguely that even seated on the desk he was still taller than she was herself.

His mouth had the firm warmth she had always expected, and she yielded to it without question. Lightly brushing her lips at first, he suddenly pressed his mouth so fiercely hard on to hers that her lips parted and her senses went spinning out of control. His hands held her relentlessly firm, with the hard palms warm through her dress, holding her against the sinewy strength of his body, and Tarin did nothing to resist, for it seemed so inevitable.

It was something she had been expecting to happen ever since those days as a schoolgirl, when she had contrived in so many ways to be wherever Darrel happened to be, just for the pleasure of seeing him. It was the culmination of all those dreams she had ever had of being wooed by Darrel Bruce and for a few moments she allowed herself to believe that they had actually come true.

It was the shrilling voice of the telephone that brought her abruptly back to reality, and she pulled away from him swiftly, as if a third person had invaded their privacy. Her eyes were wide and only half believing and she found it hard to understand how he could look so cool.

For a moment longer he still held her with his hands still spanning the slimness of her waist, then he shook his head and put one hand on the shrilling telephone, the other again reaching out, a finger stroking briefly against her neck in that gently evocative caress.

'I think we're a bit nearer burying that hatchet, don't you?' he asked softly, and smiled as he picked up the telephone while Tarin gazed at him for a moment uncomprehendingly. For a long, incredible moment she had forgotten that there was any hatchet to be buried and seeing him so easily restored to normal, her first instinct was to run away somewhere and hide for being so easily convinced there were other reasons for being kissed like that.

CHAPTER SEVEN

TARIN decided, after much thought, that the best thing to do was to forget all about the kiss Darrel had so unexpectedly given her and carry on as if nothing had happened. It was obvious that the incident had meant nothing more to him than a move towards more peaceful relations between their families, and she could hardly blame him for that, although it had been rather more disturbing than that to her.

His behaviour for the rest of the day had been no different from usual, so either he did not realise the effect he had had on her or he did not care. She preferred to think he didn't know, for she hated to think of him finding her reaction amusing, and perhaps laughing about it to himself.

She mentioned nothing to her uncle, partly because she would have found it an embarrassing subject to discuss and partly because she felt sure he would think her a complete fool for being so impressionable. Also she had a discomfiting suspicion that he would be right, for at twenty-four years old she should surely have been able to accept a kiss without being shattered to the very depths of her emotions.

The following day went fairly smoothly for her, thanks to the fact that Darrel was missing for most of the morning. He had gone off somewhere on business, so she understood, although he had had Gloria Stein in the car with him when he left, and Tarin was quite appalled to realise how much she hated the idea of them driving off together.

Whether Darrel was simply giving Gloria a lift into the nearest town Tarin had no idea, but she could not think of them together without experiencing a strangely violent dislike for the American girl. It was some time after lunch when he returned, and he seemed to be in a somewhat preoccupied mood, so that once or twice when Tarin glanced at him she wondered if something could have happened while he was out with Gloria Stein.

Mrs. Smith's arrival with afternoon tea, however, seemed to do something to restore him, and when Tarin looked across at him again briefly, he was leaning back in his chair, apparently enjoying his tea. He caught her eye and, much to her discomfiture, lowered one lid in a broad, suggestive wink which she feigned not to notice. Although the fact that he made such a gesture so soon after yesterday's episode made her feel oddly guilty.

It was much earlier than usual when he looked at his wristwatch and suggested that she finished for the day. Glancing at her own watch, Tarin frowned at him curiously, her blue eyes questioning his reason. She was a little suspicious too, she had to admit, for he was leaned back in his chair, watching her with the end of a pencil clamped between his strong teeth.

'It's rather early,' she suggested, wondering what motives lay behind the offer, 'and there's still an awful lot of work to catch up on.'

He said nothing for a moment but continued to regard her with one raised brow expressing surprise at her reluctance to leave. 'I expected you to be more than ready to leave early tonight,' he said. 'Haven't you a riding lesson this evening?'

Tarin nodded, unwilling to be reminded. 'I'm supposed to be having one,' she agreed, and that expressive brow shot swiftly upwards.

'Only supposed?'

She chanced a hasty look at the rugged face, half shadowed because he sat with his back to the light, and wondered if he realised just how reluctant she was to go on with something she had agreed to only on the spur of the moment.

'I still don't know for sure whether you've agreed to my using one of your horses,' she reminded him.

A grief glimpse of white teeth betrayed a smile and he shrugged. 'You're welcome to use any one you fancy, except Tarquin,' he told her quietly.

'Oh! Oh, I see—thank you.'

She had half hoped that he would refuse when it came to the point, and it must have been evident from her reply, for the brown eyes were watching her closely and noting her lack of enthusiasm with a faint smile. He leaned back in the big leather chair with his fingers steepled under his chin and a hint of challenge in his eyes, as if he dared her to admit she had changed her mind.

'Having second thoughts?' he suggested softly, and Tarin wished she could deny it more convincingly.

Instead she only vaguely shook her head and looked down at the letter still in her typewriter, only half finished. 'Not really,' she denied.

'And what,' he challenged with another, more definite smile, 'does that mean?'

Tarin hesitated, discomfited by his obvious amusement. 'I—I'm not sure whether I want to start so soon. You *did* suggest I might hurt my hands if I tried too soon,' she reminded him, and he nodded.

'I did.'

The brief, non-committal reply was scarcely helpful or encouraging and Tarin looked at him for a moment, mildly irritated. It had occurred to her that she might simply be using his rather offhand caution about her hands as an excuse to bolster her own reluctance, but his casual response did nothing to help her decide.

'Do—do you think I *should* change my mind?' she asked.

'It depends.' He shrugged his shoulders and another brief smile tugged at one corner of his wide mouth for a moment. 'You're the best judge of how you feel—whether you're up to it or not. How do your hands feel?'

She spread her hands in front of her and gazed down at her shiny fingertips for a second before she answered. She could quite truthfully say that they were a little sore after typing all day, but they weren't too bad, and she was reluctant to have him think she was merely making excuses.

'I don't really know,' she decided after a second or two. 'Not too bad, I suppose.'

He reached out with his own large hands across the desk, and she instinctively got to her feet and walked across the room. 'Let me see.'

Her heart was thudding heavily as she put her hands in his and they were trembling as he engulfed them in the warm strength of his hold, his long brown fingers curled about her wrists. He studied her fingertips for a moment or two, then looked up at her with such suddenness that she found herself biting her lip when she looked straight into the brown eyes.

'Why not tell Con you don't feel like riding?' he suggested.

'You—you think I should?'

It was rather unfair of her, she supposed, to put the onus of decision on to him, but she seemed incapable of coherent thought at the moment, and it would be so much easier to accept his decision instead of making her own.

'I don't propose influencing you one way or the other,' he told her. 'You know best how you feel, but if you don't want to go—then tell Con you don't.' His words denied trying to influence her, but the deep voice suggested what he wanted her to do and Tarin shrugged uneasily, all too aware of the pulsing beat at her temple and the fluttering response of her heart to his touch.

'Would—would he understand?' she queried, and a raised brow questioned her meaning.

'When he knows your hands are still painful?' he asked. 'Of course he'll understand.'

She stood looking down at her fingers for a moment, trying to decide, while Darrel still held her wrists, a curiously gentle and almost sensual pressure in the thumbs that covered her throbbing pulses. Almost as if he tried to persuade her without committing himself.

'I—I suppose he will,' she said.

'Of course he will!'

There was something hypnotic about the deep, quiet voice that for the moment mesmerised her into stillness except for the rapid and urgent beat of her heart. Then she realised with a start how near she was to allowing herself to be swayed by sheer sensual power, and pulled herself up sharply.

Her hands were not nearly bad enough to warrant calling off her date with Conrad Stein, it was simply that she was seeking excuses and was more than willing to be persuaded. What Darrel's motives were for trying to stop her going she had no idea, but she was determined to make up her own mind.

'Oh, I'll go!' she said, suddenly impatient with her own indecision.

For a moment the brown eyes held hers steadily, almost as if he knew her reasons for deciding and betraying a hint of amusement for her determination. 'You know best,' he said softly.

'I'll manage.' She was determined to sound confident, even though it was evident he was laughing to himself at her efforts. 'I don't suppose I'll need to do too much the first time, will I?'

'I don't suppose so.' He was apparently ready to relinquish his objections without too much effort, for he shrugged and released his hold on her, picking up the pencil again and twirling it round and round in his strong fingers while he looked up at her speculatively. 'I've chosen the quietest horse in the stable for you to ride,' he said quietly. 'You'll be able to manage Misty, he's as docile as a baby.'

'*You* chose him?' She blinked at him, her eyes puzzled.

'Of course,' he said quietly. 'They're my horses, remember?'

The reminder irritated her and she felt a flush of warmth in her cheeks as she stuck out her chin. Obviously he meant to have some say in her riding lessons, even if it was deciding which horse she rode. 'You *did* tell me I could have any of the horses except Tarquin,' she reminded him. 'You didn't tell me you'd already decided which one I was to have.'

'So you can,' he said. He seemed quite unperturbed by her obvious annoyance and the smile was still in his eyes as he watched her steadily. 'If you prefer not to ride Misty, you don't have to, there are plenty to choose from. I was merely trying to make sure you had a mount you could handle, that's all, and I know their temperaments better than Con does. I don't want you being too ambitious the first time out—accidents can be frightening, especially to a beginner.'

'Yes, of course.'

Tarin put a hand to her breast where her heart was thudding quite alarmingly hard, and all for nothing, she told herself ruefully, for it was simply common sense for him to choose the quietest horse in the stable for a learner rider. It had nothing to do with his making a personal choice for her, or having any special concern for her safety; he would give the same consideration to a visitor like Gloria Stein or a complete stranger.

'You don't believe me?' he asked softly, and Tarin hastily shook her head.

'Yes, of course I believe you,' she said, 'and I'm grateful for your concern, Mr. Bruce. You can't afford to have me off work again so soon.'

Her choice of words, she realised too late, was open to misinterpretation, and his eyes narrowed briefly as he looked at her. 'If you're being sarcastic——' he said, but she hastily shook her head in denial.

'I'm not,' she assured him.

'If you are,' he went on, disregarding her denial, 'you can go ahead and take Tarquin and break your beautiful neck for all I care!'

'Thank you!'

For a moment the air between them was charged with emotion, then slowly he shook his head and visibly relaxed, a dark glitter of amusement in his brown eyes. 'Very nearly another battle,' he said softly. 'There are times, Tarin McCourt, when you make me feel positively murderous!' Then he shook his head again, his mouth smiling wryly. 'Take Misty,' he said. 'You'll find him just right for you, and he's a neat little cuss too, not too big for you.'

It was so often like this, Tarin thought ruefully. She was about to lose her temper with him and he suddenly became agreeable, making it impossible for her to be angry. He knew exactly how she felt too, she felt sure, for there was still that glitter of amusement in his eyes as he sat there looking up at her steadily.

Reluctantly she met his eyes and almost at once looked down again, her pulses racing wildly as she tried to ignore the dark warmth that laughter brought to his eyes. 'I'll try not to do anything silly,' she promised, and he laughed softly.

'I'll make Con supply me with another secretary if he *lets* you do anything silly,' he told her. 'Now you'd better go and change or something—you can't go riding in that little bit of nonsense, no matter how pretty it is!'

Tarin tried to ignore the dark gaze that lingered on every curve revealed by the soft green dress she wore, and shook her head. 'If you're sure you don't need me any more today,' she said in a voice that shook despite her efforts to control it. 'I'll go and cook an early dinner, then I'll be finished in plenty of time to get ready and back here.'

'Are you scared, Tarin?'

The question was unexpected and she was half turned away to go back to her own desk, but she hesitated and looked at him with curious eyes. 'I—I don't think so,' she said. 'Do you expect me to be?'

His smile tugged crookedly at one corner of his mouth. 'With you I'm never sure,' he admitted wryly, and Tarin shook her head, suspecting he saw her as too idiotic to be capable of learning to ride and too scared to cry off.

'I don't think I'm a complete fool,' she told him. 'I should be capable of getting on and off a horse without too much trouble.'

'I didn't suggest you were a fool,' he denied with surprising candour. 'I don't for one minute believe you are, but you *are* pigheaded and I don't want you going all out to prove anything.'

'To you?' The retort was instinctive and she saw the brief tightening of his wide mouth, and the glitter that showed in his eyes for a moment as he looked at her.

'To anyone at all,' he said quietly. 'You chose to let Con Stein teach you rather than me, but that's your affair, I've no doubt you had good reasons. I just hope you don't manage to wind Con round your little finger until he doesn't know whether he's coming or going, and lets you have your head too soon.'

Tarin coloured furiously at the bland assumption he was making. He constantly made references to some imagined affair she was having with Conrad Stein, and she suspected he did it mostly to embarrass her because it gave him some sort of perverse pleasure. She found the American charming and attractive, the couple of times she had met him, but she had no desire at all at the moment to become as closely involved with him as Darrel was suggesting, and she meant to let Darrel know it.

'You have quite the wrong idea about me and Mr. Stein,' she told him in a small tight voice, and she stuck out her chin to let him know that she meant what she said.

'Have I?'

His voice was non-committal, but there was a speculative glitter in his brown eyes that challenged her, and she sighed at the almost inevitability of another quarrel. 'If you think there's anything at all between us——' she began.

'Isn't there?'

'No!' Tarin bit out the denial shortly and felt the colour flood warmly into her cheeks again as she met his eyes. 'You have no right to imply—whatever it is you're implying,' she went on in a soft, breathless voice. 'No right at all!'

'You weren't so quick to deny it last Sunday when I saw you together,' he reminded her with annoying calm, and she recalled with annoyance her own implication at that time, that he had interrupted a rendezvous with Conrad Stein. 'Also,' he went on relentlessly, 'you had no hesitation in deciding which of us you preferred as a riding instructor.'

Tarin's wide blue eyes had a glow of anger as she looked at him behind the desk, but she felt an added urgency in her heartbeat when she speculated on whether it was resentment at being passed over or some other reason that made him remark yet again on her choice.

'That really made you cross, didn't it?' she asked, without stopping to consider how rash she was being, and she hastily looked away when Darrel gazed at her for a long moment with glittering dark eyes.

'Cross?' He echoed the rather childish expression with a hint of a sneer, and she felt the colour in her face again. 'I was surprised, that's all, Tarin. I'm a qualified instructor, it's part of my job to teach beginners to ride, and I naturally expected you to accept my tuition rather than that of a—so you claim —complete stranger.'

'He *is* a stranger,' she insisted firmly. 'I've met Mr. Stein only twice before yesterday morning. Once on your driveway, a day or two after I first came here, and again at Stonebeck, when you saw us last Sunday.'

'Then your choice is even more surprising,' Darrel countered swiftly. 'You know nothing about him and yet you're ready to entrust yourself to his care out in the wilds, on your own.'

Don't *you* trust him?' she asked impulsively, and he smiled wryly, shaking his head again as he twirled the pencil he held in his long fingers.

'Not altogether, when there's a beautiful girl involved,' he told her frankly, and Tarin blinked at him for a moment, wondering if he could possibly be suggesting that she changed tutors.

'You're—you're suggesting I'd be safer with you?' she asked.

For a moment he said nothing, then he smiled faintly and looked up at her steadily, a hint of that disturbing warmth in his brown eyes. 'Don't you?' he countered softly, and Tarin shook her head, almost without thinking.

'How could I?' she asked quietly. 'History

doesn't suggest I would, does it?'

'Still harping on that same old theme!' He got to his feet, briskly impatient, and she heard her own sharp intake of breath as he came round the desk and stood for a moment looking at her before stepping back to perch himself on the desk edge with one foot swinging idly. 'You just won't bury the hatchet, will you, Tarin?'

It was partly true, she realised ruefully, although she was not entirely to blame, he must take his share too. But she could no more forget about Jeanie McCourt and Darrel's disreputable ancestor than her uncle could, when it came to the point, and yet she really wanted to break down the barrier between herself and Darrel.

She looked at him now through the thickness of her dark lashes and wondered if she would ever rid herself entirely of that girlish passion for a boy who rode like the wind over the moors and scarcely even noticed her. The darkly tanned face was so familiar to her, with its rugged features and wide mouth, and the brown eyes that could look so warm and gentle. There was still so much of the youth left in the grown man and all too much of her schoolgirl self in the grown woman.

There were so many reasons why she wanted to be on better terms with him, and yet always that indefinable something arose when she least expected it and made her say the wrong thing to antagonise him. She stood for a moment with her hands clasped together, seeking words, the right words that would heal yet another breach.

'It—it isn't all my fault,' she said at last.

'Agreed!'

His frankness made her gaze at him uncertainly

for a moment, then she shook her head. 'If it will help I'm ready to say I'm sorry,' she told him, and heard him sigh.

'I wish you meant it, Tarin,' he told her softly.

'I do!' She looked at him earnestly, her blue eyes shadowed with anxiety, her mouth softly parted as she sought for more words to convince him. 'I do mean it,' she insisted huskily. 'But you agreed it wasn't all my fault.'

He smiled faintly. 'Then I'm sorry too.'

She glanced briefly at him again and shook her head, a small frown drawing her brows together. 'I—I don't want to quarrel with you,' she confessed in a far from steady voice. 'I—I don't really know how it happens—it just does.'

'It just does!' He echoed her plaintive cry and half smiled. 'We can't help it, Tarin,' he said softly. 'I admit I try to make you angry, and I don't really know why. If you were anyone else but Tarin McCourt, and I hadn't the ghost of old Duncan at my elbow every time I'm with you, believe me I wouldn't waste time quarrelling with you!'

'Mr. Bruce——' Her voice had a husky, trembling sound to it and she could feel her heart thudding wildly in her breast as she tried to meet his eyes.

'Darrel!' She looked up at him swiftly when he corrected her in a soft, quiet voice and as swiftly looked down again when she met that dark warmth in his eyes again. 'Surely after all this time you can at least afford me the same privilege as Con Stein,' he suggested softly, and she nodded.

'Darrel,' she echoed obediently, but quite forgot what she meant to say.

'You're much too beautiful to quarrel with,' he

said in a voice that shivered along her spine like an icy finger, and a wide, slightly wolfish smile lit his rugged face, reminding her uneasily of his barbaric ancestors. 'I'm especially fond of brunettes,' he told her. 'Brunettes with big, beautiful blue eyes.'

Tarin's heart was beating so hard she felt oddly breathless, but she fought wildly against the almost irresistible urge she had to go to him and run her fingers through the thick, reddish hair that flopped over his forehead, and to hug close to the strong, bruising hardness of his body. His brown eyes had a bright glitter that should have warned her how foolhardy it would be to do anything so rash, and she resisted her own impulses determinedly.

'Mr. Bruce—Darrel——' She tried hard to re-member what it was she wanted to say to him, but shook her head when it eluded her again.

'Come here!' He spoke softly and when she looked at him she saw that the strong brown arms were extended towards her and his long hands curved invitingly. She shook her head slowly, more in pleading than in denial, but the hands beckoned irresistibly. 'Tarin?'

'Mr. Bruce——'

'Will you come here?' he insisted softly, that glint of wickedness still lighting his brown eyes, and she moved towards him almost without realis-ing she was doing it.

His arms closed round her, gently at first, then with an insistent strength that drew her against the warm, hard leanness of his body, moulding her softness to him, unresisting as yet, and still dazed, and his mouth just touched hers lightly. One hand, reaching up, took the thickness of her dark hair in his fingers and twined it tightly as he pulled back her head.

Tarin felt herself sway even closer, her hands spreading slowly over the broad warmth of his chest, sliding over the smoothness of his shirt, pressing her sensitive palms to the hard urgency of his body. His mouth took hers fiercely, raising a small cry from her before she yielded to its compelling demands and slid her arms up round his neck.

It was some seconds before Tarin realised that the door had opened behind her, and she gasped audibly as she drew back, her mouth still pulsing warmly from his kiss. Darrel released her slowly, but his bland self-control stunned her like a cold shock, and she wished only for the floor to open up and swallow her before she need face the newcomer.

'Hello, Gloria.' He sounded so matter-of-fact that Tarin could scarcely believe her ears, and she dared not turn round yet and let the American girl see how flustered and disconcerted she was. 'I presume you had a reason for coming in?' he asked, and Tarin could easily imagine the expression on Gloria Stein's beautifully made-up face.

'You little bitch!'

The voice sounded alarmingly close, and Tarin swung round swiftly to find the other girl just behind her, her thin face flushed with anger and her pale blue eyes glittering like chips of ice. Tarin would have moved away, out of reach of the clawing fingers she half expected to feel on her cheeks, but she was still held by Darrel's hand on her arm.

'That's enough, Gloria!'

His voice sounded so remarkably cool and calm in contrast to her own chaotic emotions that Tarin felt a moment of intense hatred for him as she looked at those rugged, unperturbed features. It was possible to guess, from his manner, that this was not the first time he had been in such a situation, and the realisation only added to Tarin's humiliation.

She remembered too late Conrad Stein's hints at a less than angelic reputation, and that dark glitter in his eyes should have warned her too, but she had chosen to ignore both and allowed herself to be swept along in the urgent chaos of emotions he could so easily arouse in her. Gloria Stein obviously despised her for being just another easy conquest, another silly girl ready to succumb to the stark, primitive attraction of Darrel Bruce, but Gloria Stein's contempt was nothing compared to the contempt Tarin felt for her own weakness. Twice in two days was lesson enough for anyone.

'You just couldn't resist it, could you?' Gloria Stein's anger was still directed entirely at Tarin, and she stood only inches away from her with her long thin hands clenched tightly as she glared her dislike from those icy eyes.

'Oh, for God's sake leave it, Gloria!' Darrel told her impatiently. He slid from the edge of the desk and released his hold on Tarin's arm at last, not in the least embarrassed, but impatient with the blonde girl's jealousy. 'Stop making mountains out of molehills,' he told her. 'You know as well as I do how these things happen—it's no good blaming Tarin!'

His defence of her, his easy dismissal of the incident only served to make Tarin feel worse, and she clenched her hands tightly as Gloria Stein renewed her attack.

'I didn't see her objecting!' Gloria snapped angrily, and her clenched hands looked as if she meant to strike out at any moment. 'She knows what she's up to, the little bitch!'

'Miss Stein——' Tarin began, but a second later gasped into silence when a vicious slap stung her cheek sharply and made her head spin for a moment.

'Tarin, I'm sorry!'

His apology, like his defence, only angered her more and she winced as from another blow when he put a hand to her face and gently stroked her cheek where the red fingermarks already stood out plainly. His regret was seemingly genuine, but Tarin was too humiliated to allow any such gesture of repentance, no matter how genuine it might be, and she drew away from him hastily, her blue eyes sparkling with anger and tears of humiliation.

'Don't!' she cried sharply.

Turning away from him, she hurried across to her desk and blindly grabbed her handbag, not bothering about the letter still in the typewriter, almost running to the door. She turned in the doorway, drawn by some inexplicable force, and looked back at him standing tall and angry beside his own desk with Gloria Stein close by, hard and brittle and just as angry, her blonde head thrown back in a gesture of defiance.

'Tarin, wait!' Darrel strode across the room before she could get through the door and a strong hand grasped her wrist, preventing any further move on her part. 'Don't go off in a temper, or you'll do something you'll regret!'

'I've already done something I regret, Mr. Bruce,' she said in a small throaty voice that threatened to break at any moment. 'I shouldn't have come for this job, but I don't intend staying long enough to regret anything else!' She looked down at the strong brown fingers curled around her wrist relentlessly, and shook her head. 'Now will you please let go of my arm and allow me to go home?'

'You'll be here in the morning?'

Tarin hesitated before she answered. Strictly speaking he was entitled to her services for at least another week, but she was very unsure she could face another week in his company without much the same thing happening again, and she couldn't bear that.

'I—I don't think so,' she said huskily, and the fingers on her wrist tightened their hold.

'I think you will,' he said quietly. 'You can't just walk out on me like that. Your last boss may have let you get away with it, but I shan't—you be here in the morning, Tarin, or I'll come and fetch you!'

It appalled her to feel the way her heart leapt when he issued the ultimatum, and she could scarcely see for the pulses that throbbed wildly in her temple when she looked at him through her lashes, remembering how, only minutes ago, she had yielded to his kisses so willingly.

Tall, strong and, at the moment, savagely angry, she could still see him as belonging to another, less civilised age, and she shivered involuntarily. Even his hair looked redder, more like those bearded savages out there in the hall, and his rugged features were set stubbornly, the brown eyes glittering. Suddenly she felt she knew exactly how Jeanie McCourt had felt all those years ago, and she found the realisation strangely exhilarating.

'I suppose you *are* entitled to a week's notice,'

she allowed, husky-voiced. 'Very well, Mr. Bruce, I'll be here in the morning, but please take a week's notice as from then.'

The brown eyes glittered down at her and again his fingers squeezed her wrist tightly. 'Don't be a little hothead,' he said in a voice that was obviously meant to be inaudible to Gloria Stein, who still stood, hard-eyed and suspicious, by the desk. 'Think it over, Tarin, and decide in the morning.'

'I've already decided,' she declared firmly, and made no effort to keep her voice down. 'I'm leaving, Mr. Bruce, and you won't persuade me otherwise!'

'Then go to hell, you obstinate, pigheaded McCourt!' he told her in a fierce, strong voice, and his fingers crushed her wrist so hard she gasped and made futile efforts to prise herself free. 'Get to hell out of here, and don't bother coming back!'

'I thought you were coming to fetch me if I didn't serve my time!' The retort was irresistible and she managed at last to ease the cruel grip on her arm, glaring at him with bright, dark blue eyes. 'Make up your mind and I'll know whether or not to bar my door!'

To her intense surprise, he laughed, a short, hard but definitely amused laugh, and she felt her fingers curl into her palms at the sound of it. 'A barred door didn't stop Duncan Bruce,' he told her, his eyes glinting with challenge. 'It won't stop me if I want to come for you! You bar your door, you little hellcat, and see how much good it does you!'

Tarin's heart was thudding wildly and her eyes were a dark, glowing blue, bright, like the colour in her cheeks, stirred by some strange sense of ex-

citement she had never known before. 'You bar-
barian!' she told him, in a surprisingly quiet voice.
'You're no better than your disreputable ancestors
—but believe me, I've no intention of becoming
another Jeanie McCourt!'

His eyes, glittering and dark below the craggy
brows, actually glowed with laughter and his teeth
gleamed briefly in the rugged brown face as he
leered down at her, deliberately threatening, as if
he was enjoying the whole thing. Which he probably was, Tarin thought ruefully, for her own
heart was hammering breathlessly hard as she met
that challenging gaze and felt herself trembling.

'You want to bet?' he asked softly.

Tarin thought seriously about not going back to
Deepwater to meet Conrad Stein, later that same
evening, but she did not quite see how she could
avoid going when he was expecting her and she had
no way of letting him know except by ringing
Deepwater, and that she was loath to do.

Her preoccupation during dinner had not es-
caped her uncle's notice and she was not surprised
when he remarked on it at last.

'Is something wrong?' he asked, and Tarin
smiled ruefully.

'Nothing unexpected,' she told him. 'I've just
had a slight difference of opinion with my boss,
that's all.'

She hesitated to say how serious the latest disagreement had been or that she had given notice to
leave, for deep down she still had doubts that she
would actually want to leave when it came to the
point. Darrel Bruce could play as much havoc with
her adult self as ever he had when she was a school-

girl, and she might as well admit, if only to herself, that she would find it very hard to go away again.

Her uncle eyed her for a moment with a curiously speculative look in his eyes. Wondering if there was any chance of her making the break with Darrel, she suspected ruefully—if only he knew how near he was to having his way! 'Do you not get along as well as you thought you would?' he asked, and Tarin shrugged.

'We don't get along too badly,' she said. 'Not considering all things. After all, we've two hundred years of that ridiculous feud to live down, and it isn't easy.'

'He'll no be an easy man to work for,' her uncle guessed, and again Tarin shrugged, uwilling to place the entire blame on to Darrel, no matter what he had done to anger her.

'I've had worse bosses,' she said non-committally, and Robert McCourt frowned.

'You'll surely never get the Bruce to behave like a civilised man,' he declared with certainty.

Tarin unthinkingly put a hand to her mouth where Darrel had recently shown just how uncivilised he could be, and she half smiled as she looked out of the window at the tree-girded mass of Deepwater. 'I have hopes,' she told him softly. 'Though I'm not sure I can stand the pace.'

'But if——' Her uncle broke off short and frowned at the telephone jangling shrilly in the small hallway. Then he got up to answer it and Tarin, for some inexplicable reason, felt her heart racing like a wild thing in her breast as she followed him with her eyes to the door.

She heard him give a brief identification then he listened for a few seconds before turning his head in her direction. 'Do you not want to speak to her?' he asked, and the caller apparently answered in the negative, for he shrugged and a few seconds later returned the receiver to its base and came back into the dining-room.

Tarin looked at him curiously, her heart still thudding rapidly as she questioned him. 'Something important?' she asked, and her uncle eyed her for a second before he answered.

'It depends how much importance you attached to your riding lesson with that American at Deepwater,' he told her. 'He's been called to an important meeting, so he says, something to do with the hotel, and he can't see you as he'd arranged. He asked me to apologise for him and says he'll try and see you tomorrow.'

'Not if Darrel Bruce has anything to do with it, he won't!' Tarin said softly, and for some reason she did not quite understand, felt like laughing suddenly. 'Oh, Darrel knows how to get his own way,' she said, disregarding her uncle's frown of curiosity. 'I don't know what Con Stein has to do with the running of the hotel, but I should have known that if Darrel decided I wasn't going to ride with him he'd find some way of stopping me, however devious!'

Robert McCourt sat down at the table again and his frown showed that, regardless of her own view of it, he did not find the situation amusing in the least. 'He's not the right to decide who you see or don't see, surely?' he said. 'What gives him the right, Tarin?'

She shrugged, her heart pounding heavily as she poured herself more coffee, and trying not to smile or even laugh aloud. There was a strange, singing sense of excitement stirring in her blood, and she made no attempt to find a reason for it.

'Maybe he thinks two hundred years of tradition and having Duncan Bruce for an ancestor gives him the right,' she said softly.

CHAPTER EIGHT

TARIN found the prospect of another day at Deepwater rather daunting after her emotional departure yesterday. She had said little during breakfast and she was aware that her uncle was watching her curiously while they ate their meal, probably speculating on the reason for her silence. Fortunately he had said nothing, for she did not feel like explaining her uncertain future at the moment, partly because she had the idea that once she had told her uncle about her giving Darrel notice to leave, her position would be irrevocable.

What her current feeling for Darrel was, she dared not even guess at the moment, but she was ready to admit that it was something more potent than the innocence of girlish fancy it had started out as. He was a very attractive man, there was no doubt at all about that, as there was no doubt that she was neither the first nor the last woman to find him so.

What his feelings were for her, she was even less sure, but she guessed they were completely superficial and went no further than an office flirtation, or at most a brief affair, neither of which prospect gave her much comfort. Whether Gloria Stein had any more serious claim on him, she didn't know, and that was likely to be another complication that would have to be faced sooner or later.

If only she had enough common sense to pack up and go, there and then, she would probably save herself a great deal of heartache, but for the moment she couldn't bring herself to do anything so definite.

Perhaps Darrel had been right, she had behaved like a hothead last evening, storming out as she had, though it did not excuse him saying so the way he had. It would do no harm, however, to at least think about it further while she walked to work.

She had decided to risk defying the roll of scudding grey cloud that came in threateningly over the hills, and set off without a coat, for it was warm despite the threat of rain, and walking would soon make her even warmer.

The misty, early-hours look of the surrounding hills never failed to enchant her, and she smiled to herself as she looked across to where the little stream glinted softly in Stonebeck's green hollow and the rowans stirred sleepily in the light morning wind.

Torin Brae swept up from the edge of the tiny village, patched with the dark growth of budding heather, and sat with a circlet of grey cloud around its brow, while the tiny but beautiful waters of Torin Fall fell like liquid silver down its side to join with the deep waters of the little loch. There was something so peaceful and lovely about it that Tarin knew she would find it hard to leave again, even had there been no other reason for staying.

It looked peaceful now, and soft and gentle, but she knew that in the winter, with the cold winds blowing in off the mountain snows, it could be bleak and savage; and there was something much the same about the man who was still very much on her mind as she made her way along the cobbled road through the village. Darrel Bruce too had moments of warmth and gentleness, but he could also be savagely hurtful. A man who, in his way, could be as dangerous as the country he belonged to.

The light wind did no more than stir the trees along the carriageway into a soft whisper of sound as she passed beneath them, her hair wisping softly against her face and neck. It had a damp, warm feel to it, as if it already carried the beginning of the threatened rain.

Facing Darrel again would be something of a challenge, she was forced to admit, and the nearer she got to Deepwater the less sure she was that she would be able to stick to her avowed intention of leaving in a week's time. It was possible, of course, that Darrel had meant what he said when he told her to go and not come back, in which case the decision was out of her hands, but somehow she believed his outburst last evening had been no more binding than her own.

She turned another bend in the carriageway and it occurred to her for the first time to wonder what would have happened if she had decided to stay at home today. Whether or not he would have come looking for her, as he had threatened.

The memory of the threat brought a rueful smile to her lips and she admitted to herself for the first time that she found the idea more exciting than frightening. Her uncle, however, would have been both shocked and horrified to have the Bruce, as he always called him, banging on their door and demanding that his niece come out or he'd come in for her. What the rest of the village would have made of it did not bear thinking about, but she still smiled to herself when she thought of it. It was a pity in a way that she had not had the forethought to put him to the test.

Her preoccupation deafened her, as it had once before, to the sound of anyone approaching from behind and, as on that occasion, the first indication she had of danger, was the sound of Darrel's voice cursing roundly, both her and his startled horse. He had been coming fast, of course, and with Tarin jut out of sight round the next bend, he was forced to pull up his speeding mount too hastily, so that the startled animal's reaction almost unseated him.

There was a flurry of words and movement for several moments while he fought to retain control, and she hastily stepped out of danger, sparing a moment to admire yet again, his confident handling of the situation. A combination of firmness and gentleness, of curses and soothing words soon had the spirited animal in hand again and he looked down at her at last with a hint of resignation.

'I might have known it was you again!' he said shortly. 'Damn it, Tarin, don't you ever walk properly to the side of the road?'

Determined not to be drawn into a disagreement with him so soon in the day, Tarin looked up at him with an expression as polite and calm as she could muster in the circumstances. 'Good morning, Mr. Bruce,' she said quietly.

It was not easy to sound so cool and matter-of-fact when every nerve in her body responded to him so violently, and she could no longer pretend to be surprised at the effect he had on her senses. It was something she was forced to accept as inevitable, no matter how foolish she knew it to be. If this initial meeting was an omen for the rest of the day there was little likelihood of his suggesting that she stay on, and she already felt a little cold corner in her heart at the prospect of going away.

He wore close-fitting blue jeans this morning that clung to his long, muscular legs and made them look even longer. A navy cotton shirt gave added darkness to his tanned face and neck and fitted snugly across the broad chest, his brown arms, below rolled sleeves, smoothly powerful as he kept the restless horse under control.

His reddish-brown hair was untidily windblown after his ride and once again Tarin experienced the almost irresistible urge to run her fingers through its thick roughness, and to press her hands to that broad chest while he held her close in his arms. Realising at last how her emotions were running away with her, she pulled herself up sharply and looked up to find him eyeing her quizzically.

'So formal?' he asked softly, and Tarin controlled the thudding beat of her heart only with difficulty.

He surely couldn't have forgotten so soon or so easily what had happened yesterday, and yet he seemed genuinely surprised at the formality of her greeting. Surely he couldn't be so insensitive as not to realise how humiliated she had felt when she fled from the room without even stopping to do the various little jobs that were normally part of an automatic routine.

She glanced up at him briefly and met the challenging gaze of the brown eyes warily. 'Have you forgotten that I gave you a week's notice yesterday?' she asked.

He obviously found the recollection amusing, for he cocked one brow at her as he once more brought the shifting stallion relentlessly under control. 'Oh yes, your dramatic little exit! I naturally expected you to have recovered your senses, having slept on it!'

Tarin stood there on the carriageway, feeling quite minute in contrast to the sleek enormity of his mount. What he said was near enough to the truth to make her uneasy, and she preferred not to meet his eyes again. 'I don't see why you should expect me to have second thoughts,' she told him huskily, seeing herself already lost. 'I had every reason to act as I did.'

She could guess, even without looking at him, that one craggy brow would be quizzing her again. 'What reason?' he asked bluntly. 'Because I kissed you? Good grief, you little prissy, you've been kissed before, certainly!'

She could feel herself blushing like a schoolgirl, and the realisation angered her. What right had he to embarrass her, to make her feel as gauchely uneasy as ever she had ten years ago? The only purpose it served, apart from making her angry, was to make up her mind for her at last that her last night's decision had been the right one. By behaving as he was, Darrel was simply making it easier for her to stand by her decision to leave.

'It wasn't only because you—because I was kissed,' she denied as calmly as she could. 'You know it wasn't, Mr. Bruce.'

'Well, I can't think of any other reason,' he declared bluntly.

'Can't you?' Her voice had an uncharacteristically hard edge to it, but it was better than have it shake and tremble as it was threatening to do. 'You have a very short memory, Mr. Bruce!'

He pulled the restless Tarquin round firmly. 'You mean Gloria coming in?' he asked. 'It was a pity about that, but you surely don't think *that* was my fault! I'm sorry she slapped you, but I didn't do that either, and you didn't need to act as if it was the end of the world and go storming off the way you did!'

'Oh, you wouldn't understand!' Tarin cried in exasperation. 'I—I felt—humiliated being found like that!'

'For heaven's sake, why?' he demanded. 'Haven't you been caught kissing the boss before?'

'Certainly not!' She hated his bringing it down to crude basics like that and she glared at him indignantly, her blue eyes blazing. 'And certainly not when their—their girl-friends are the ones who come in unexpectedly! It was obvious Miss Stein was furious—and heaven knows what cause you've given her to think she has the right to be furious!'

That had been rash of her, she realised. He was quiet for a moment, too quiet, she thought ruefully, and waited for the inevitable retaliation. 'You assume a great deal,' he said at last, and sounded surprisingly calm, despite the harshness of his voice, so that Tarin chanced an upward glance through her lashes. Knowing him as intimately as she appeared to surely gave Gloria Stein some claim to his affections, especially after all the years they had known one another.

'I know you've——' she began, attempting to explain her meaning, but one large hand waved her impatiently to silence.

'You don't know!' he denied harshly, then looked pointedly at his wristwatch. 'And you've wasted enough time out here, it's time you were at your desk—there's plenty for you to do!'

'But I wanted you to know——'

He pulled his horse round again, hard, and looked at her briefly over his shoulder as he applied his riding crop smartly to the animal's glossy hide. 'Be there!' he said harshly.

Tarin watched him go with a sense of dismay, for there was surely little chance now of his wanting to keep her on as his secretary, and she felt almost tearful as she made her way towards the house in the wake of the racing Tarquin. It was only a matter of days now and she would have to pack her bags and leave her uncle's house to go back south. Home to the uncertainty of job-hunting.

She was just about to go in through the front doors when she heard someone call from behind her. 'Hey, Tarin!'

She turned swiftly at the sound of the now familiar voice, and faced Conrad Stein with mixed feelings. No doubt he had had good reason for not seeing her last night, but she could not help feeling a little cool towards him when she felt so sure it was because he had allowed Darrel to influence him.

She was also anxious not to waste further time talking with him when she had been so brusquely ordered to be at her desk. Certain civilities, however, had to be observed and she smiled at him politely as he came up the steps two at a time and smiled at her as he opened the door, stepping back to allow her through first.

'Good morning,' she said, and he fell into step beside her as she crossed the big hall, his fingers touching her bare arm tentatively.

'I'm sorry about last night, Tarin, truly I am.'

She shook her head, only thankful that he had no

idea how reluctant she had been to ride with him. 'It really didn't matter,' she assured him.

'There'll be other times, huh?'

He looked as if he had no doubt at all about her willingness to make another date with him and she felt rather guilty as she shook her head. 'I don't think so, Con,' she said. 'I'm—I'm leaving Deepwater, you see, next week—it wouldn't be worth starting riding lessons when I'm going so soon.'

'Leaving?' His hand encircled her arm, bringing her to a halt just outside the office door. 'But why, for heaven's sake?'

Tarin shrugged, conscious of the need not to waste any more time in talking to him when she knew that Darrel was on the other side of the door, impatient and unrelenting. 'It's rather a long story,' she told Conrad resignedly. 'And it's much better that I go—I shouldn't really have come in the first place.'

'The old Bruce–McCourt feud?' He looked as if he found it hard to believe. 'But surely things like that don't go on in this day and age! I can't believe it!'

'Oh, it isn't really that,' Tarin denied, uneasily aware that at least some of their words must be audible to Darrel. 'Anyway, the reason doesn't really matter—I'm leaving and that's an end to it.' She looked at him and smiled a little ruefully. 'I'm sorry about the riding lessons, Con—it could have been fun.'

'It would have,' he assured her. 'And I don't pretend I'm not disappointed.'

Tarin found curiosity uppermost for the moment, and she looked at him through the thickness of her lashes as she speculated on the reason he had given for not seeing her last night. She would not have dared question Darrel on anything so personal, but Conrad Stein was somewhat less awesome, and she banished tact in favour of sheer curiosity for the moment.

'You told my uncle you had to attend an unexpected meeting last night,' she ventured, and he nodded. Tarin laughed, as if to dismiss an unlikely rumour. 'He got hold of the wrong end of the stick when he passed on the message,' she told him. 'He said it was something to do with the hotel!'

'That's right,' he said. 'We have an interest, you might say!'

Her heart was tapping away suddenly at her ribs, agitatedly, as the first discomfiting suspicions entered her head and refused to be dismissed. 'Deepwater?' she asked in a small voice. 'You have an interest in Deepwater?' He nodded his head again, his eyes more shrewd suddenly, and she stared at him in disbelief. 'But—but I thought Deepwater was Darrel's. I mean, *really* his—it's always belonged to the Bruces!' Unable to grasp the truth of it, she looked around her at the portrayed faces of Darrel's fierce, redheaded ancestors, then shook her head in confusion and disbelief. 'It's been theirs for hundreds of years!'

'Right!' he said, and she almost believed it was malice that gleamed in the depths of his grey eyes as he studied her reaction. 'Only things are a little different now, honey. These days they can't go pillaging and looting all over the countryside to pay for the upkeep! These days they either marry money or borrow it!'

Tarin swallowed hard and there was a small, cold sensation in her stomach suddenly as she looked at him. 'And Darrel?' she asked huskily.

Conrad laughed, a harsh-sounding snort of satisfaction, as if he enjoyed the situation. 'He borrowed from the Stein millions,' he told her with cruel candour, 'but he'll probably have to do the other thing to stay afloat—I know Gloria's hoping he does!'

Tarin's head was spinning with confusion and she could not even bear to contemplate the idea of Darrel marrying Gloria Stein simply to keep Deepwater out of trouble. The Darrel she thought she knew would not do it, but she was no longer very sure of anything, and she faced the fact that he would do a great deal to keep his home. That he would even consider taking the step that Conrad Stein suggested gave her a sickening feeling in the pit of her stomach.

'I—I had no idea things were so bad,' she said, and her voice had a small tight sound to it, so that he looked at her narrow-eyed.

It was not difficult to understand the barely concealed dislike he had shown for Darrel in their last couple of meetings, for it was certain Darrel would make an uneasy partner in such an arrangement as theirs. It would also account for Gloria Stein's air of possessiveness—she probably saw no way out for him but to marry her if he was to keep his home.

'You don't know the half of it!' Conrad informed her, and again laughed, as if the situation amused him. 'But to give him his due, he's clever— he's damned clever, and tricky! Smarter than we gave him credit for, I guess!'

Tarin looked at him curiously, no longer pretending that it was of little interest to her, but remembering all those other business interests of

Darrel's and wondering if the Steins knew any-thing about them, or if Conrad was simply guess-ing.

Darrel had instructed her that all correspond-ence from the accountant was to go straight to him and she was allowed to do no more than open the envelopes, but even that little had given her some inkling that the Bruce fortunes were quite healthy. Maybe his partners in the hotel were less well in-formed and only now began to realise that he was more solvent than they had suspected. Perhaps last night's meeting had enlightened them, hence Con-rad's manner this morning.

'I—I must go,' she said, suddenly very unwilling to discuss it any further, and she moved to the door on legs that trembled alarmingly.

He seemed willing enough to let the subject drop, but looked at her enquiringly as she put a hand on the door-knob. 'Will I see you tonight?'

The question took her by surprise and for a moment she simply stared at him, then she shook her head slowly. 'I—I don't think so, Mr. Stein.'

He recognised the formality of his surname with a raised brow and for the first time Tarin realised how much her attitude had changed towards him in the past few minutes. When he first spoke to her, a few minutes ago, he had been just a charming and attractive American whom she was unlikely ever to see again once she left Deepwater; now he was a threat to Darrel's future and she felt a dis-tinct and definite antagonism towards him. It was a change that she recognised ruefully, and she won-dered how Darrel would have taken it, had he known.

'Mr. Stein?' he echoed. 'What's wrong, honey?

Aren't you on my side any longer?'

'I—I'm not on anyone's side,' Tarin denied, and wished with all her heart that she had not stopped to talk to him. 'I'm just a bit surprised—a bit confused to learn about Deepwater, that's all.'

'You don't like the idea of it changing hands?' he guessed, and the glint in his grey eyes was less friendly than it normally was.

'I didn't say that,' she argued. 'And it hasn't actually changed hands, has it? Darrel still has an interest, in fact if he's only borrowed the money, as you said, he'll be able to pay it back and——'

'And you're hoping he will be able to pay it back?' he guessed softly. He shook his head and there was a small crooked smile on his mouth as he looked at her speculatively for a second or two. 'Don't waste your time and sympathy on Darrel Bruce, honey,' he advised, 'you don't stand an earthly! The only way he'll get out of the wood for keeps is by marrying Gloria, and no matter what gallant manners you attribute to him, he'll do it to keep Deepwater, don't you worry!'

'I—I don't believe it!'

Her voice was dry and harsh and Tarin licked her lips with the tip of her tongue as she desperately sought to convince herself she was right about Darrel. But Conrad Stein was even more sure of his theory and he shook his head with an air of certainty that dismayed her.

'I've no doubt he finds the idea of romancing a secretary as pretty as you kind of doing what comes naturally, honey,' he told her, 'but you don't have a couple of million dollars in the bank, do you, Tarin? Gloria has—and with Darrel that's what counts at the moment!'

'Oh, but——' She shook her head rapidly, then, without saying another word, turned and opened the door behind her and went in, a bright flush of colour in her cheeks and a suspiciously bright mistiness in her eyes.

She kept her back to the room for a second or two while she made some attempt to recover her self-control. Not only had she betrayed to Conrad Stein whose side she was on, but also just how she felt about Darrel, and she prayed that he would not see the necessity to pass on the information. That would make her position impossible.

Darrel was sitting behind his desk when she moved at last, his brows drawn together into a frown. He had not yet changed out of the clothes he wore for riding and she noticed again how untidy his hair was. It fell in a thick, reddish-brown thatch half across his forehead and looked just right above the aggressive cragginess of his features.

Looking at him briefly through the thickness of her lashes, she experienced a strange new tenderness and realised for the first time just how much he did mean to her, a realisation that did little to comfort her at the moment.

Surely, she thought, no hotel owner and manager had ever looked so disreputably untidy or so nerve-tinglingly attractive at the same time. Deepwater was his home and, no matter if he was obliged by circumstances to entertain paying guests there, he made few concessions as far as his own way of life was concerned.

'You took your time!' he said gruffly as she moved away from the door, and Tarin bit her lip.

In contrast to her own feelings his harshness was almost unbearable, and without saying a word she hurried across to her own desk. She put her handbag in the desk drawer and rolled the incomplete letter she had left last night out from the platen so that she could start it afresh. Little, ordinary jobs that she could do with little or no concentration. It was appalling to realise how near to tears she was and she hoped to heaven she wasn't going to make a complete fool of herself, and cry.

'Tarin?'

Something in her manner must have told him that all was not well with her and he got up from his desk and came across to her, while she attempted to look busy. For a moment he stood on the far side of her desk, looking at her curiously, then he came round and stood right over her, playing havoc again with her senses when the warmth of his nearness enveloped her.

He perched on the edge of her desk and one hand reached down to gently raise her chin until he could study her face with its bright cheeks and blue eyes, hidden below dark lashes. 'What's Con said that's upset you?' he asked quietly, and a small, wry smile quirked one corner of his mouth as he guessed she was about to deny that he had told her anything. 'I know you've been talking to him out there,' he told her. 'I wasn't listening, so I don't know what he's been regaling you with, but it must be something you regard as pretty earth-shattering, judging by your expression. You *are* a little dramatist, aren't you?'

'I just told him I was leaving you at the beginning of next week,' she said, seeking a safer subject than his own personal affairs.

'Leaving me?' He laughed softly and shook his head, while his thumb slid with caressing gentle-

149

ness over her jaw. 'You sound more like a runaway wife than a departing secretary!'

'Oh, I didn't mean——' She bit her lip when she met the warmth of those brown eyes, and hastily looked away again. 'You know what I mean,' she finished lamely, and he sighed.

'I wish I did,' he confessed. 'I thought you'd have straightened that out in your cock-eyed little mind by this morning.'

'I told you earlier, Mr. Bruce——'

The large hand cupping her chin lifted her face, while the thumb moved gently over her soft skin. 'Why are you so bent on leaving me, Tarin?' he asked softly.

It took her several seconds to find the right words to answer him and before she did she reached up and eased his hold on her, moving her head so that he no longer supported her chin. 'I—I think it's for the best,' she said at last.

'Something Con told you?' He gave her no time to answer, but there was a hint of granite in that firm, strong voice. 'Did he tell you I was broke?' he demanded, and the blunt harshness of the question so stunned her that for a moment she stared at him with wide and disbelieving eyes, then she shook her head. 'No, of course he didn't!' she denied.

'Of course he didn't!' He echoed the words softly. 'Oh, I know he would if he thought it would work,' he went on, still in the same soft but certain voice. 'Only you wouldn't desert the sinking ship, would you, Tarin?'

She flushed, her eyes suspiciously bright when she detected sarcasm in the question. She thought how ready she had been to defend him, how unwilling to believe that he would marry for money, even to save Deepwater. His harshness hurt, and she curled her hands tightly as she looked up at him.

'No, as it happens, I wouldn't,' she said in a small, tight voice, 'but it's obvious you don't believe it, Mr. Bruce. Not that it applies in this case, because you're *not* a sinking ship!'

'You sound pretty sure about that!'

Tarin hesitated. Her conscience was clear, but she suspected he would not believe that either. 'I open your post,' she reminded him. 'I don't read it, of course, not the reports from the accountant, but I don't have to to know that you're a pretty successful investor.'

'And you've told Con Stein that?'

She stared at him unbelievingly, her heart hammering breathtakingly hard at her ribs, realising at last what he was getting at. He suspected her of passing on confidential information to Con Stein, of letting his not altogether trusting partners know how he really stood financially, and his mistrust of her hurt more than anything he had said or done so far.

'You—you know I wouldn't,' she whispered huskily. 'You surely know I wouldn't do that!'

'I hope you wouldn't,' he said softly, and after a second's hesitation, shook his head slowly. 'No, I don't think you would.'

Tarin looked up at him, her blue eyes accusing. 'I thought you trusted me,' she said bitterly. 'You said the McCourts were honest, no matter what else they weren't—now you only *think* I am! So much for your trust!'

'Tarin——'

'Don't touch me!' She twisted her head sharply

out of his reach when he would have touched her cheek again, and looked at him with bright, angry eyes, her mouth trembling. She held her hands tight and curled in her lap and her voice had a shaky, unsteady sound as she spoke. 'Maybe you judge everyone else by your own standards,' she told him shakily. 'But you're wrong about me, Mr. Bruce—*I* know when to draw the line and there are things I *wouldn't* stoop to!'

'Oh?' He was quiet for a long moment, then he reached down and pulled her to her feet, which brought her much too close to him for comfort. He was taut and angry and there was a kind of tense excitement about him that communicated itself to her. 'You'd better explain,' he said quietly.

'Let me go!' Her attempt to free herself only brought her in contact with him and she shivered when she brushed the hard firmness of his thigh.

'Not until you tell me what the hell you're talking about,' he said implacably.

'I don't have to tell you anything!' She was desperate to escape now, and almost panicking when he pulled her even closer and looked at the softness of her mouth with an intensity that made her shiver.

'Do I have to use my own methods of making you talk?' he asked softly, and she shook her head hastily. If he kissed her now she would not only tell him everything that Conrad Stein had said to her, but her own position would again be in doubt.

'If you—if you kiss me I'll—I'll scream for help,' she said in a small and strangely quivery voice, and to her intense mortification, Darrel laughed.

'No one's ever done that before,' he admitted frankly, and shook his head slowly. 'I'm beginning

152

to think you really *are* a little prissy, Tarin Mc Court!'

'I'm not a prissy,' Tarin denied, swiftly on the defensive and feeling rather childishly gauche as she bore his frank and speculative scrutiny. The brown eyes went slowly over her from the top of her dark brown head to the soft curves revealed by a brief pale pink dress that clung lovingly to every one of them. 'And don't look at me like that!'

'Oh, I'd like to do a great deal more than look!' he threatened softly, and his hands on her arms tightened so that she gave a gasp of apprehension and tried to pull free.

'You—you two-faced, double dealing——'

'Hey!' He was laughing again and she wished she had the cool nerve to slap him hard, but her legs felt too trembly and weak as she stood there with his hands curled tightly about her arms and the hard, lean warmth of his body just touching her. 'What have I done to deserve such a trouncing?' he demanded, and Tarin glared at him resentfully.

'I'd have thought you were afraid of losing your insurance!' she told him in a small, tight voice, recklessly frank because she had to do something to break his hold on her.

The strong brown fingers tightened still more and he pulled her right up close to him so that his craggy face was only inches away, the brown eyes glitteringly bright and challenging. 'Explain!' he ordered softly.

'I don't have to!'

'Oh yes, you do!' he insisted softly. 'I'm getting a little tired of dropped hints. Let's have the—whatever it is I'm supposed to have done—out in the open, shall we?'

Tarin licked dry lips, seeing no way out of it now that he had brought them so far. 'Miss Stein,' she said, and he raised a brow curiously.

'Gloria?' he said quietly. 'What about her?'

'Oh, you know well enough!' she declared, wishing she was a hundred miles away and that she had never seen Darrel Bruce again. 'Con Stein told me——'

'Ah!'

His brief expression of understanding made her bite her lip and if he had not shaken her and made it evident that she could not back out now, she would have said no more. 'He—Mr. Stein says—he told me that you'll marry his sister—Miss Stein, because——'

She did come to a stop there because she saw the glint that came into his eyes at that point, as if he guessed what she was going to say next. 'Go on!'

He looked inexorable and Tarin felt herself shaking all over as she walked into the trap she had set for herself by being so reckless. She stood with her eyes downcast, but knew he was watching her with those relentless eyes and his fingers were tight and hard round her upper arms.

'You'll need her to keep Deepwater—to keep the house out of debt,' she said in a small, trembling voice.

'I see.' The hands on her arms did not lessen their hold, but the thumbs slid back and forth slowly in a way that was at once caressing and threatening. 'And you believed what he told you, did you, Tarin?'

If he had been furiously angry it would have been easier to bear, Tarin told herself, but his cool, quiet response made her feel more guiltily uneasy than ever, and she dared not look up at him for fear of what she might see in his eyes.

'Look at me!' One hand jerked her head up sharply and she found herself looking into the brown eyes whether she wanted to or not, finding them almost black in his anger and glittering like dark liquid as he made her look at him. 'So,' he said softly, 'you see me as a sort of male gold-digger, do you? I marry Gloria and then, when I'm presumably nicely set for life, I carry on as if nothing had happened while Gloria lets me do as I like rather than lose me—is that your idea? Yours and Con's, presumably, since he put it into your head!'

'I didn't—I mean, I——'

'You believed it!' he insisted harshly, and again he jerked her face up, forcing her to look at him. 'Well, thank you, my faithful little fan club—I'm flattered!'

'I *didn't* believe it!' Tarin cried despairingly. She felt close to tears again and it was obvious that he would never believe the truth now.

His eyes glittered down at her and there was a hard look about his wide mouth. 'Well, for your information,' he went on as if she had never spoken, 'you're doing not only me an injustice but Gloria too. I don't need to marry for money, as it happens, but I wouldn't even if I *did* need to, I haven't sunk that low yet; and Gloria isn't the kind of woman to sit back and let anyone else play fast and loose with her property. That *is* how you saw me, isn't it?' he asked harshly.

Tarin was too near to tears to answer for a moment, she could only shake her head and she had never felt so utterly miserable in her life before.

'I'm sorry,' was all she could manage after several seconds of silence, but he was in no mood to be tolerant, and his hands gripped her arms tightly as he looked down at her with that hard glitter in his eyes.

'Don't be,' he told her harshly. 'I'm only sorry I've proved such a disappointment to you after all these years. It must be very disillusioning to discover your idol has feet of clay; but maybe it'll teach you not to put a mere man on a pedestal again, Tarin.' He got up from the edge of her desk and stood for a second looking down at her in silence. 'Maybe you'd better go when your time's up,' he said softly. 'I'm not sure I trust myself not to do something very violent about you, Tarin—and we don't want history repeating itself, do we?'

CHAPTER NINE

THE temptation not to go back to Deepwater the following Monday morning was almost irresistible. All the week-end Tarin had been more than usually quiet and subdued, and it was inevitable that sooner or later her uncle would notice and comment. Not only was her own imminent departure making her unhappy, but the thought of Darrel having to resort to borrowing, or even worse, eventually, to keep his precious Deepwater, troubled her more than she cared to admit.

She had avoided going anywhere at all during the week-end, even for her customary walks, in case she met either Darrel or Conrad Stein. Darrel she wanted to avoid in case she made a fool of herself yet again by begging him to let her stay on, as she felt sure she was bound to do given any encouragement at all, and her feelings about Conrad Stein and his sister owning part of Deepwater, whether temporarily or not, she was afraid might make her less than friendly towards him.

Monday proved to be, rather ironically, a lovely bright, soft morning, the kind of day when she should have been lighthearted and carefree, and she probably would have been if she had not been so reckless in her dealings with Darrel. Instead she felt as if the weight of the whole world was on her shoulders, and there was a sad, dark look in her blue eyes that did not go unnoticed.

As she expected her uncle noticed and commented, although he did manage to remain silent about it until breakfast time on Monday. Watching her toy with her rapidly cooling breakfast, he shook his head over her lack of appetite, unable to remain quiet any longer.

'Have you no fancy for your breakfast, Tarin?' he asked, and she looked across at him and shook her head.

'I'm not hungry,' she confessed. 'It's—it's a bit warm this morning, I've never a very good appetite when the weather's warm.'

'It's not as warm as it has been,' her uncle decreed firmly, and looked at her again with a curious look in his eyes. 'Is there something troubling you, girl?'

It would be wonderful, Tarin thought, to be able to tell someone about how she felt. Someone who would understand, not blame either her or Darrel for what had happened, but be able to give a clear, logical picture and enable her to as well. Her uncle was biased in her favour, so he was not the best one to unburden to, but he was at hand and she did need someone.

She was appalled to find herself so close to tears, ready to sob out her troubles to anyone who would listen. All week-end long she had nursed her aching heart and soon she must tell someone or make a complete and utter fool of herself, she felt sure. Much better to console herself with a comforting weep now than have it happen when she was closeted in the office with Darrel.

She looked across at him and pulled a wry face, unaware of just how close the tears looked in her misty blue eyes. 'Does it show?' she asked, with an attempt at levity, and Robert shook his head.

'You've looked unhappy all the week-end, my

dear,' he told her. 'I wasn't going to say anything, but—well, I hate to see you like this.'

'It's—it's nothing anyone can do anything about.'

Almost as if he knew what lay behind her unhappiness, Robert looked at her shrewdly for a moment before he spoke. 'Have you settled your differences with Darrel Bruce yet?' he asked.

Tarin shook her head, her teeth biting hard into her bottom lip. 'It's unlikely I ever will now,' she said, and laughed shakily as she shook her head. 'I've—I've been a complete idiot and made him—made him hate me!'

The tears came at last and she was unable to stem the flood that poured down her cheeks, no matter how she tried. In a moment her uncle was out of his seat and round beside her, a comforting arm about her shoulders. He thrust a large handkerchief into her hand and made gentle soothing noises as he consoled her.

'There now, lassie,' he said kindly. 'Don't cry about it, for it surely can't be so bad, now can it?'

Tarin nodded her head miserably, mopping her streaming eyes with his handkerchief and wishing to heaven she could exert more control over herself. Robert was bound to blame Darrel for the state she was in and she could not, in all fairness, blame him for it all. True, he had refused to let her apologise, but that was only in keeping with his natural arrogance as the Bruce and in her present mood she could not blame him for it.

'It's just about as bad as it can be,' she told Robert dejectedly. 'And—and it was all my fault!'

'Now I can't believe that,' Robert insisted firmly. 'I've no doubt there are two sides to the question.'

'There always are,' Tarin offered with a watery smile. 'But unfortunately I always seem to be on the losing side.'

'What's he done to you?' She saw the way he frowned and tried to recover enough breath to enlighten him before he became too angry. 'If that savage has hurt you,' he declared fiercely, 'I'll see that he pays for it!'

'Oh, Robert, it—it isn't as easy as that!'

His fierce determination for revenge was not altogether unexpected because it was Darrel Bruce who was involved. Even before he knew exactly what was troubling her he was ready to blame Darrel, simply because he was who he was. Her uncle, she realised, saw her as yet another injured innocent wronged by the Bruces—another Jeanie McCourt—and he probably even relished the situation. All he needed was an excuse to go up to Deepwater and settle with the current owner once and for all.

'He'll not get away with it!' Robert insisted. 'Whatever it is he's done, he'll not get away with it!'

Tarin shook her head slowly, trying to impress him with how wrong he was. 'Darrel's not getting away with anything, Robert,' she assured him. She dried her eyes again and tried to keep them from filling with tears again, but even thinking about leaving Deepwater and Darrel so soon made her cry and she bit her lip desperately, trying to stop the threatened storm. 'It's—it's all my fault,' she insisted shakily. 'It really is, Robert.'

She had never felt so utterly dejected in her life before, and there seemed to be nothing she could do to put things right. It was doubtful if Darrel was

160

even prepared to listen to her, however abjectly she apologised, and certainly her uncle's solution was unlikely to help. If only she had kept quiet about Gloria Stein she might still be Darrel's secretary instead of crying her heart out because she would probably never see him again.

'I can't believe it,' Robert argued stubbornly. 'You're not a hard girl to get along with, Tarin, and——'

'Neither is Darrel—unless you happen to be a McCourt,' she told him bitterly. 'Oh, Robert, why do I have to say the wrong thing always?'

Her uncle looked at her curiously and the temptation to tell him everything was irresistible. '*Do* you always say the wrong thing?' he asked, and she nodded ruefully, biting back a great sigh that shuddered through her.

'Always,' she said huskily. 'We've—we've tried so hard to—to put an end to this silly feud thing, Robert, but always there's something that drives us on.' She shrugged her shoulders helplessly. 'Perhaps Darrel's right—our past, our upbringing is against us at every turn. We always quarrel, no matter what good intentions we have, it's as if we couldn't help ourselves.'

'And it matters?'

Robert's brown eyes had a shrewd but kindly look and for a moment their brown colour reminded her of Darrel's so that she was once more blinded with tears. 'It matters,' she admitted frankly. 'To me at least, not so much to Darrel, I think.'

'Oh, Tarin, Tarin, had you no more sense, lassie, than to fall in love with the Bruce?'

Her uncle hugged her close for a second and she

closed her eyes against the exquisite agony of realising how much Darrel meant to her, and how helpless it was to expect him to do anything other than despise her after what she had said to him yesterday.

'I wish I had!' She looked up at him and impatiently brushed the tears from her eyes with one hand. 'I thought I could cope with things,' she went on ruefully, 'and while it was no more than the old schoolgirl crush, I could. But now——' She shrugged and her uncle shook his head slowly, obviously unhappy about the unexpected turn things had taken.

'It's not been very long, Tarin,' he reminded her. 'Are you sure you're not just attracted to a very virile and forceful man with whom you've been in close proximity for several weeks?'

'I'm pretty sure.'

The certainty in her own mind rather surprised her, but she really had no doubt at all that what she felt for Darrel was something far more deep than a mere passing fascination for a very attractive man. The thought of his despising her the way he undoubtedly did at the moment made her deeply unhappy, and she could do nothing to control the fresh tears that ran down her cheeks dismally.

'Oh, my poor lassie!' Robert hugged her close, shaking his head over her misery. 'What *are* you going to do, my dear?'

'I've already given him notice,' Tarin confessed miserably. 'Thursday, after we quarrelled.'

'Ah!' He nodded wisely. 'So that was what was wrong!'

'Then on Friday morning we almost——' she bit her lip in the anguish of knowing it had been her own fault that the peace moves had not come to fruition. 'I didn't see him again all day, not even before I came home, and now it's too late.' She shook her head despairingly. 'I leave later this week.'

'Had that American anything to do with it?' Robert asked, and she looked up at him for a moment before nodding her head.

'I suppose so, in a way,' she said. 'Con—Conrad Stein, the American, told me that Darrel would inevitably marry Con's sister Gloria sooner or later, because he needs a rich wife to keep solvent.'

'And you believed him?'

Something in his tone made Tarin frown at him curiously. If he had simply nodded his head and said it was no more than he expected of the Bruce, she would not have been surprised. But his current reaction puzzled her.

'I didn't really believe him,' she denied, and found herself slightly on the defensive, which was another puzzling thing in the circumstances. 'I—I told Con Stein I didn't believe it, but I—oh, I don't know how it happened! I suppose I just couldn't resist taking a dig at Darrel about it and he thought—he's convinced, that I believe it of him!'

'Oh, Tarin, you silly girl!' Her uncle was shaking his head and, difficult as she found to believe it, she was sure that his reaction was much the same as Darrel's had been. 'Had you no more sense,' he asked, 'than to say such a thing to a man like Darrel Bruce?'

'No, I hadn't,' she confessed miserably. 'And you can guess the result!'

'Did you not realise that he'd not do such a

thing?' Robert was firmly confident he was right, and Tarin stared at him for a moment in disbelief.

'*You* don't think he would?'

'I know he wouldn't,' he affirmed, and there was a bright gleam of certainty in his eyes that was somehow reassuring.

'But you always said——'

'I've always said a lot about the Bruces,' he admitted with an air of getting something off his chest, 'but I've never truthfully met any of them the way I have this man. Even so, I'd never see them as men who would sell themselves for an easy life.' For a moment she detected a gleam of ironic amusement in his eyes as he looked down at her steadily. 'Oh aye, they'd maybe steal a pretty girl and carry her off against the will of her family, but they'd not demean themselves by marrying for money, and if you suggested they might, then I'm not surprised he's finished with you!'

'Uncle Robert!'

It was quite a speech in the circumstances and for several moments Tarin stared at him unbelievingly, then she shook her head, unable to find words to express her surprise. Robert McCourt allowed a brief and very wry smile to touch his mouth for a moment as he looked down at her. 'You never thought to hear me say good about a Bruce, I'll bet,' he guessed, and she detected a definite hint of defiance in the way he said it that made her smile, despite the way she felt.

'I never did,' she admitted.

'Well—maybe I've been a bit hasty at times in my judgment,' Robert went on, and looked faintly embarrassed as he rubbed one hand over the back of his head while he made the confession. 'Maybe I could have been wrong about them on some counts.' He looked directly at her suddenly and there was a fierceness about his brown eyes that almost matched that of Darrel's red-bearded ancestors. 'That's not to say they haven't been a pack of savages,' he declared forcefully, 'but they're men for all that, and—well, maybe this one's better than they've produced for a long time.'

'Maybe,' Tarin echoed softly, and he nodded his head, as if he had suddenly made up his mind about something.

'If you want this young blood,' he told her with embarrassing frankness, 'then you shall have him, lassie! Even if I've to kidnap him the way his barbaric ancestor did our Jeanie!'

Tarin suddenly felt less unhappy and miserable, more optimistic as she looked up at her uncle's strong and determined expression. She could even make an effort at laughing as she mopped the last of the tears from her eyes with his handkerchief.

'You'd never manage to capture Darrel Bruce,' she told him. 'Not even with an army!'

Robert studied her for a moment, kindly but speculative, as if he sensed her change of mood. 'Then you go and get him in your own way, my girl,' he told her softly. 'You can if you've a mind to!'

'I doubt it,' Tarin denied ruefully, and shook her head, horribly uncertain again for the moment. 'You don't know Darrel, Robert. You didn't see the —the way he hated me for suggesting he might be ready to marry Gloria Stein to save Deepwater.'

'If you've enough love for him, you'll find a way,' her uncle told her quietly. 'I'd a lot of opposition from her family when I married Margaret, but I loved her and I meant to have her.'

Tarin looked at him for a moment in surprise. 'I didn't know that,' she said. 'I suppose it never occurred to me.'

'We married very quietly,' Robert said with a smile for the memory that was so dear to him. 'But I had my Margaret and that was all that mattered to me. I didn't want a big fuss and nor did Margaret, bless her heart.'

'It was a long time ago,' Tarin said softly, and impulsively squeezed the hand that still rested on her shoulder. 'I was too small to remember anything about it.'

'No one came,' he said quietly. 'There was just Margaret and me and a couple of friends. Doctor Robertson was one, and the minister, of course.'

'In the little village church?' Tarin asked, and he nodded.

'Where she is now,' he said softly.

For several moments Tarin sat thinking about the aunt whose memory she did not always recall very clearly, then she shook herself and looked at her uncle, wiping the last traces of tears from her eyes. 'It sounds very romantic,' she said at last, 'but there's a difference, Robert. You and Margaret loved one another—with me——' She shrugged uneasily. 'I don't think I have much chance with Darrel. I can't even see myself being given the opportunity to apologise or anything else.' She looked at him for a second, remembering some of his first words on the subject of Darrel Bruce. 'You said yourself he's a hard man,' she reminded him.

'So I did,' Robert allowed, 'but not so hard he wasn't concerned when you burnt your hands.'

'Oh, that!' She shrugged once more and half

smiled. 'I think he was more concerned then that he shouldn't be without a secretary than for any other reason.' Getting no response to that allegation, she hurried on. 'I was debating whether or not to go in at all this morning,' she told him.

'But surely you will,' Robert told her. 'It would be silly not to, Tarin!'

She made a wry face and nodded. 'Yes, I suppose it would,' she admitted. 'But I'm not looking forward to facing Darrel again this morning.'

'Maybe he guesses you'll feel like that and he won't expect you,' Robert suggested. 'If he does then you should go in, just to show him you're not so easily deterred.'

'Show the McCourt banner?' Tarin suggested with a faint smile, and he nodded. 'Yes, I suppose you're right, Robert.' She sighed deeply and got up from the table. 'I'll go in, though heaven knows what kind of a day I can expect!'

Tarin's feelings were somewhat mixed when she discovered that she had the office to herself. It was a relief in one way and yet she would have welcomed an opportunity to try and apologise for yesterday. There was plenty for her to do, and she set about dealing with the morning's mail before finishing some letters left from yesterday.

There was another letter from his accountant in the now familiar cream-coloured envelope and another from New York with the title Fennelly and Lucas heavily emblazoned across the envelope as well as the contents. Curiosity almost got the better of her as she put the envelopes to one side and laid the letters neatly one on top of the other on the spotless blotter where Darrel could easily find them, but she determinedly averted her eyes and gave her attention to the rest of the mail.

When the door opened behind her she became quite still for a moment, feeling her heart plunge into rapid activity and her cheeks colour warmly. She turned slowly, some letters still in her hand, a greeting ready on her lips, determinedly composed, at least outwardly. 'Good morning, Mr.——' She spoke as she turned, then stared in disbelief at the man who stood in the doorway.

Conrad Stein's thin, boyish figure was clad in riding gear and his grey eyes looked across at her curiously for a moment, as if he speculated on the kind of welcome he was to get. 'Tarin?' He hesitated a moment longer, then stepped into the room. 'Hi!'

'Good morning, Mr. Stein.'

She turned back and tapped the pile of letters she held on the edge of Darrel's desk to straighten them. Remembering how Darrel had so determinedly kept him out of the office before, she doubted if it would do her own case much good for him to find the American there with her now, and she tried to impress him with how busy she was, hoping he would take the hint and go.

But discouragement, she realised, did little to deter Conrad Stein and he closed the door behind him and came across the room towards her. 'Can't I beg forgiveness?' he asked quietly, and Tarin felt bound to look at him at least.

'You haven't any need to, have you, Mr. Stein?' she said as coolly as she could. 'You saw yourself in the right, and your insults *were* mainly directed at Mr. Bruce, weren't they?'

'Ouch!' His rueful grimace was so comical that she almost laughed, and there was an almost irresistibly boyish look about him this morning that made her wonder if she could possibly have imagined yesterday's malice. He came and put a hand on her arm, his fingers firm but not hard, and smiled at her hopefully. 'Have a heart, Tarin,' he begged. 'I'm truly sorry I upset you yesterday.'

'About maligning Dar—Mr. Bruce?' she asked quietly, and for a second she saw a hint of that malicious hardness in his eyes again.

'It's yet to be proved that I did malign him,' he pointed out. 'But I am sorry I involved you in it, especially when you're——' He possibly took warning from her straight look that forbade him to mention her vulnerability where Darrel was concerned. 'Anyway, I wanted you to know how sorry I am,' he went on.

Tarin took the letters across to her own desk, leaving him to follow, if he chose to, although she would far rather he left before there was any danger of Darrel coming in and finding him there. 'You know I'm leaving this week, Mr. Stein,' she reminded him quietly. 'It isn't worth worrying about petty differences, is it?'

Conrad's rather cool grey eyes studied her for a few moments and he frowned. 'You're still going?' he asked. 'I thought you would have sorted that out with Darrel during the day.'

'He wasn't here,' she said shortly, and wondered at the brief puzzled frown he gave.

'Oh?'

Obviously his absence had been unknown to at least one of his partners and she wondered if she had inadvertently given something away that Darrel would rather have had kept quiet. 'I don't think he liked the idea of being with me all day,' she told him in an attempt to cover up, but it was obvious he didn't believe it.

'Tarin!' A long thin hand reached across the top of the typewriter and prevented her from doing anything, his thin body bent forward so that his face was close to hers. 'Don't stay mad at me,' he begged. 'Be nice, honey, please!'

'Mr. Stein——'

'Con! For heaven's sake, what do I have to do to get near you?'

'I'm sorry.' Tarin realised at last that she was probably being unreasonably unfriendly and she leaned back in her chair and looked up at him with a faint smile. 'But I'm not very happy about you being here,' she confessed. 'If Mr. Bruce finds you——'

'He'll throw me out!' he admitted with a grin. 'So come with me for a couple of minutes where he can't see us!'

'I hardly think——' she began, but he grabbed her by the hand and pulled her to her feet.

'Aw, come on!' he encouraged. 'Darrel won't go searching for you if you're missing from the office for a couple of minutes.'

'But I have——'

'It'll keep!' he asserted forcefully, and pulled her towards the door without giving her time to object further.

She started in surprise when she saw Gloria Stein crossing the hall, and half expected her to object to the company her brother was keeping, but instead she merely gave them a brief, rather satisfied smile and seemed not at all surprised. Conrad lowered one eyelid briefly at his sister, then pulled Tarin along after him, across the hall and out through the rear door, past the kitchens.

'Where are you taking me?' she asked, unwilling to go too far in case Darrel came back and found her missing. 'Mr. Stein——'

'Con,' he insisted, and stopped just outside the door, leaning against the sunwarmed wall of the house, his hands holding both of hers, his grey eyes glistening down at her.

'I really shouldn't be here,' she objected, casting uneasy glances round the stone-cobbled yard that spanned the distance between the back of the house and the stables. 'If Mr. Bruce comes in and finds me missing——'

'He won't,' Conrad assured her with a grin. 'He rode over early to see some guy about a pony he's buying, and when Darrel starts talking horseflesh he's unstoppable.'

Tarin looked across at the squat, stone-built stables where a groom went busily about his chores and completely ignored them. If Darrel was on horseback then he would inevitably come into this yard sooner or later, and once more she shifted uneasily. 'Just the same,' she said, 'I'm not sure I should have left the office with no one there.'

'Professional secrets?' he teased, and laughed at her worried frown. 'Take it easy,' he said. 'His secrets are safe enough!'

Tarin was remembering the letter from the accountant and the other from New York, both of which Darrel would hate to have in unauthorised hands, and shook her head uneasily. 'There were some letters——' she began, then hastily recalled that Darrel would almost certainly not want his partners to know about them in view of the seeming distrust between them, and shook her head. 'I shouldn't have left the office unattended,' she said. 'I must get back, Mr. Stein—Con.'

He still held her hands and made no move to release her or to change his rather indolent position against the wall of the house. 'Don't fret so much,' he told her. 'You're leaving this week, so why should you worry who walks in and reads his letters?'

'Of course I do!' She pulled her hands free and looked at him for a moment with reproachful blue eyes. 'I'm still responsible for the office when Darrel isn't there, and I couldn't——'

It was almost as if mentioning his name had brought him into view, and Tarin's heart lurched anxiously when she saw the familiar figure coming through the rear entrance into the stable yard. She spared not another glance for Conrad Stein, but gave a breathless little gasp of realisation and ran swiftly in through the back door of the house before she was spotted.

There were a couple of guests in the hall as she sped across it to the office and once again Gloria Stein appeared as if from nowhere just before she reached the office door. The blonde woman's eyes took in her breathless and anxious state and she smiled meaningly, one brow raised as if in comment.

'While the cat's away?' she remarked softly, as Tarin hurried past her, and Tarin felt the colour warm her cheeks at the misinterpretation.

She felt short of breath and angry with herself for letting Conrad Stein persuade her, and she took no time to think before she spoke. 'The cat's back!' she retorted. 'And you're quite wrong about my reason for hurrying, Miss Stein!'

There was no time to hear what Gloria's reply might be, so Tarin simply opened the office door and hurried across to her own desk, taking up the letters she had discarded. Her heart was hammering at her ribs until she could scarcely breathe and she sorted through the letters she held for several minutes without seeing them, until the door opened at last and she looked up sharply when Darrel came in.

He looked lean and hard in fawn trousers and shirt and he still carried a riding crop, tapping it against one long leg as he strode across to his desk, then flinging it into a corner. He said nothing, and she might just as well not have been there for all the notice he took of her.

The past forty-eight hours, she decided ruefully, had done little to sweeten his mood, and her heart sank as she debated whether or not to speak first. Perhaps he had decided to ignore her altogether for her last few days, and at the thought of his actually doing so she bit her lip again anxiously.

'Mr. Bruce.'

She licked her dry lips nervously as he turned and fixed her with a steady dark-eyed look of enquiry that could not have been more cool. If she had hoped for some sign of relenting this morning she was disappointed, and her heart was as heavy as lead as she tried to appear cool and controlled when she faced him.

'Yes, Miss McCourt?'

His formality banished any reasonable excuse she had had for addressing him and she hastily avoided his eyes as she desperately sought for something to say. 'I—there were two confidential letters in the mail this morning,' she managed at last, and for a brief moment she could have sworn that a familiar glint of warmth showed in his eyes.

Then he turned and looked down at the top of his desk with a frown. 'Are there?' he asked coolly. 'Then where have you put them?'

'Why, on your desk!' She stared at him uncomprehendingly for several seconds, then hastily got to her feet and half ran across the room, her heart clamouring wildly in panic. Sure enough the blank purity of the blotter was unburdened by any sign of letters and her eyes were wide with with dismay when she looked up at him appealingly. 'But—they *were* there,' she whispered huskily. 'I put them there myself.'

She had never seen those brown eyes so coldly condemning before and he towered over her like a relentless figure of vengeance, his craggy face as fierce as any of those painted ones out in the hall.

'Maybe you left them with Con Stein in your haste to get back here before I spotted you,' he suggested softly, and Tarin closed her eyes and put her hands to her mouth to stifle the cry that rose to her lips.

It seemed like an eternity before she drew another breath, and Darrel neither moved nor spoke, so that the silence eventually became unbearable and she opened her eyes. He still stood there, less than a couple of feet away, looking grimly unrelenting, and she bit her lip so hard that she almost drew blood.

'I—I put them there,' she insisted in a small husky voice that trembled dismayingly. 'I *did*, Darrel, and I—I wouldn't show them to anyone else, you must know I wouldn't.'

Her eyes in the smooth oval of her face looked

huge and childlike as she begged for his trust, and she dared to hope she saw a glimpse of warmth at last in the brown eyes, although he showed no signs of it in his face. The craggy features looked dark and forbidding and she could feel the agitated flutter of her pulses as she faced him.

'Then where are they?' he asked again. 'Letters don't just walk away, and these were very important ones.'

'I—I know.'

She was recalling the past fifteen minutes in every detail. Coming into the office, opening the post and laying those precious letters on his desk— then Conrad Stein had come in. She had been more or less compelled to go with him out into the yard at the back of the house, passing Gloria on the way, but she had been gone no more than five minutes, Gloria Stein could confirm that. Realisation came to her with stunning clarity suddenly, and she gave an audible gasp, one hand covering her mouth.

'Miss Stein,' she whispered without hesitation. 'I passed Miss Stein going out *and* coming back, she could have——'

'Quite likely,' Darrel said grimly. 'And by now they'll know I can get Deepwater out of trouble.'

Tarin was puzzled by his attitude. If he was solvent enough to get Deepwater into his own hands again, surely her own minor misdemeanour was unimportant, and yet he was looking just as fierce as ever. 'But isn't that what you wanted?' she asked, looking at him with wide, puzzled eyes, and his top lip curled scornfully for a moment as he looked down at her.

'Of course it's what I want, you little idiot,' he said harshly. 'But unless I move fast I've probably lost it now—thanks to you!'

Tarin stared at him in disbelief, her heart thudding heavily in her breast and the tears she had shed earlier threatening to appear again as she swallowed his harsh judgment. 'I—I didn't know,' she whispered huskily. 'I didn't——'

He swung round again swiftly and impatiently, lifting the telephone and giving the operator a number in a short, angry voice, while Tarin spared only a moment to stare at his broad, unrelenting back before she fled from the room without even stopping to close the door behind her.

CHAPTER TEN

'I SHOULDN'T have gone back again,' Tarin said miserably. 'I knew I shouldn't have gone, and—and now I've made things a hundred times worse. I let Conrad Stein persuade me to leave the office when I shouldn't have done—I shouldn't have left the office unattended.'

'So that his sister could take those letters?' her uncle suggested, and Tarin nodded. 'You think he knew what she meant to do?'

Tarin shook her head, not sure of anything any more. 'I don't know,' she confessed dismally. 'He might have done or he might really have wanted to talk to me—I just don't know.'

She felt drained of emotion, so unhappy that she could think of nothing at the moment except that she would never be going back to Deepwater again now. Maybe Mrs. Smith would see that her handbag was returned to her—she had not even stopped to collect it on her way out—or perhaps one of the other staff members would bring it for her. Being in Darrel's bad books almost inevitably meant being in Mrs. Smith's too—certainly she would be unlikely ever to see Darrel again.

She looked up at her uncle where he sat perched on the edge of a low table in the sitting-room, a consoling hand holding hers, his good-looking face wearing an expression of mingled regret and speculation. 'I've made a real mess of things, haven't I?' she asked dolefully, and was unable to do anything about the sudden mistiness that blurred her vision.

'Oh, it couldn't have been all your fault, my dear,' Robert conceded gently. 'Circumstances were against you from the start, and then the fact that the American girl had her sights set squarely on young Bruce didn't help matters.'

Tarin managed to smile wryly. 'My one consolation,' she confessed ruefully, 'is that Gloria Stein won't be getting what she wants either, and I can't help feeling glad about that, even if it is spiteful of me!'

'Only human, my dear,' Robert told her with a faint smile. 'Only human, that's all.'

It was a warm, bright afternoon, and normally Tarin would have been just leaving Deepwater to come home. Instead she was already busying herself preparing the evening meal, trying not to think about the disturbing events of the morning, and her sudden flight from the office.

Now that it was all over she realised just how much there was that she would miss by going back south. Not only the wonderful scenery and the sense of independence it gave her living away from home, but being near Darrel and able to see him every day. He had been right—she was a hothead who acted without thinking.

Even just thinking about him again was enough to bring those persistent tears to her eyes and she impatiently brushed them away with the back of one hand before resuming her potato-peeling. It was high time that she faced the fact that Darrel Bruce was not for her—her grown-up dreams of sharing his life had stood no more chance of becoming reality than her schoolgirl ones had.

As a rule her uncle came home for his dinner

about six o'clock, but she took little notice when he had not arrived by ten minutes past. The meal would keep hot quite easily and it was quite possible he had been delayed by some small crisis at the works. By six-thirty, however, she began to wonder what had become of him, and at twenty-five minutes to seven she rang his office to see if he had left.

Her answer came from a gateman-cum-watchman who was the only one left on the premises, and he informed her that Mr. McCourt had left at his usual time. Worried at last, Tarin was just beginning to seriously consider what she should do next when he arrived, and she looked at him curiously when he hugged her with unusual enthusiasm as he came in.

'I'm sorry I'm so late, my dear,' he told her, 'but I—well, to be honest I bumped into Darrel Bruce just after I left for home and we've had a wee talk.'

'Oh! Oh, I see!'

Tarin wished there was something she could do about the rapid beat of her heart and the pulses that pounded so heavily against her temple that she could scarcely hear her own voice, let alone Robert's. She couldn't bear to think of him quarrelling with Darrel on her account, although it did not sound as if they had quarrelled. A 'wee talk' could mean almost anything, and she was almost as reluctant to imagine him pleading with Darrel on her behalf as she was to think of them quarrelling.

'I'll tell you about it at dinner,' Robert decided before she could question his meaning, and gave her a small, consoling pat on her shoulder as she went into the kitchen to dish up their delayed meal.

'What did you have to say to one another?' she asked a few moments later. 'You—you didn't say anything to him about—did you, Robert?'

'Of course I said something to him, my dear,' Robert told her gently. 'One cannot talk to a man without saying something.'

'Oh, you know what I mean,' Tarin insisted with an impatient shake of her head. Somehow she felt that he was playing for time, and the suspicion made her uneasy as to his reasons.

Her uncle carefully swallowed a mouthful of braised lamb and nodded his approval before enlightening her, and she wondered if she had ever felt so much like being rude to him before. 'When you've had your meal,' he said at last, 'how about walking down to Deepwater, Tarin? He wants to see you.'

Tarin stared at him, her eyes wide and so darkly blue they looked almost black and frankly disbelieving. 'I—I can't do that,' she said huskily. 'I couldn't, Robert, he only wants to make my leaving official—let me know he doesn't even want me to work out my notice. I couldn't see him again and—and pretend it didn't matter that I—that I'll never see him again! I can't, Robert, I really can't!'

'There, there, lassie!' He reached over and patted her hand gently. 'You'll feel better about things when you've had your dinner.'

Tarin looked at him reproachfully although she said nothing. It was too bad of him to sound as if it was all nicely cleared up and that once she had seen Darrel and collected her things there was nothing else to worry about. It wasn't as easy as that, and he should realise it.

He had not admitted to approaching the younger man first, but she had a strong suspicion that was what had happened and she could imagine what Darrel had made of that. Probably thinking she had got her uncle to speak up for her and try and persuade him to take her back as his secretary.

Robert, she realised ruefully, was more impressed with Darrel than he would have been prepared to admit. He had grudgingly allowed a certain liking after their first meeting, and further acquaintance seemed to have confirmed his impression.

'I heard the full story,' he told her after a moment or two, and apparently taking her interest for granted. 'As that other fellow told you, young Bruce borrowed money to put Deepwater back on its feet. He was very frank about everything, and I admired him for it; in the circumstances he realised I'd be interested.'

'He wanted you to know just how close I came to ruining everything for him,' Tarin said bitterly. 'I don't blame him if you were making excuses for me.'

'He was to pay back the loan in a lump sum within four years,' Robert went on, ignoring her interruption, 'that was the written agreement he had with the Steins. Being life-long acquaintances of theirs they allowed him a further six months' grace on top of that—a verbal agreement and therefore not binding in law like the first one. Legally they could have foreclosed and taken over Deepwater nearly three months ago.'

'Oh, I see!' She gazed at him anxiously, wondering just how damaging her own part had been.

'Apparently the Steins had no idea about his

other business activities until quite recently and it never occurred to them that he was on the brink of repaying the loan and getting Deepwater back.'

'I—I suspected they might not know,' Tarin admitted, shaking her head. 'And I shouldn't have left those letters there while I let Con Stein persuade me to go outside with him.' She looked at him with wide, anxious eyes close to tears again. 'Oh, Robert, please tell me I didn't lose Deepwater for him!'

'You've no need to worry about that,' Robert assured her with a wry smile. 'He wasted no time— he had the money paid over straight away and, once the formalities are settled, Deepwater's his again.'

'Oh, thank God!' Tarin closed her eyes, the tears escaping as she pushed away her half-eaten meal. 'It could have been disastrous,' she said in a small, shaky voice. 'Gloria Stein *wanted* him to be in debt to them—to her at least, Con admitted as much. If she'd been able to claim Deepwater——' She shivered at the future Darrel might have had to endure with his home gone. 'He really would have hated me then. As it is——' She shrugged, glad at least that Darrel's dream was solid reality at last.

'As it is, my dear, you'll go and see him, will you not?' Robert suggested softly, but Tarin shook her head.

'I—I can't, Robert.' It took all the courage she possessed to say it, but she thought she knew exactly how Darrel would be feeling. 'He'll—he'll never trust me again, and—and I can't blame him.'

'Tarin——'

'It's better this way,' she insisted, trying vainly to

182

dispel the tears that once more blinded her. 'We—we fight all the time, and—and it's mostly my fault. It—it's no use trying to undo something that's been going on for over two hundred years. Maybe some time in the future the McCourts and the Bruces will be able to get along, but—but it won't work for Darrel and me.'

Robert said nothing for a moment, but even through her tears she noticed his apparent unconcern for her unhappiness and felt hurt by it. 'I'd not like to cross that young man myself,' he said softly. 'He's a mind of his own and he——' He shrugged with apparent resignation. 'Ah well, I suppose you know best, lassie.'

It was most unusual for her uncle to go out during the evening, but Tarin was too wrapped up in her own unhappiness to realise that anything untoward was happening. He was simply going to walk down into the village and visit Doctor Robertson, he told her, not as a doctor but as an old friend.

If she was to leave soon there were plenty of things she could do and Tarin spent some time sorting her belongings ready to be packed. She had no idea how the time had flown and when she heard a car stop outside she was surprised to find it was already after nine o'clock.

A peep out of her bedroom window made her gasp audibly and draw hastily back, for the sleek black car parked outside the gate was all too easily recognisable. There was no sign of the driver at the moment, but she felt her whole body shaking like a leaf as she stood there behind the concealing curtains, almost holding her breath and wondering what on earth she could do.

The door bell chimed below in the hall and she drew another sharp breath, but made no move to go and answer it, her legs were much too weak to carry her that far. Why he was there she did not even stop to consider, she was much too busy trying to cope with a veritable storm of emotions that made her heart beat like a steam hammer in her breast and curled her hands into tight little fists.

'Tarin!'

The voice was unmistakable, and she shook her head as if he could see her doing so, one hand to her mouth when she heard the bell sound, shrilly impatient, again. She heard his footsteps on the path and then his voice raised again and sounding quite angry.

'Tarin! I know you're there, you little idiot—open the door!'

The mild insult finally moved her and she leaned half out of the window and looked down on him. His reddish head was untidy as usual and the strong, broad shoulders looked wider than ever from this angle, a white shirt stretched across them, open at the neck as always and showing that tanned column of neck and throat with a pulse at its base that made him seem unexpectedly vulnerable.

'Tarin!' He sounded increasingly impatient, and her heart gave a wild lurch when she heard a distinct thud on the front door. 'Damn you, will you answer me?'

'No!'

She did not realise how futile her answer sounded until she saw him step back, and the faint but definite smile on his wide mouth as he looked up at her. The brown eyes had a deep, dark, glowing look, but she was ready to believe that it was anger that made them so.

His feet were planted firmly apart on her uncle's rather ragged patch of lawn and those powerful arms were akimbo, his big hands set firmly on his hips. 'What did you say?' he asked, with surprising quiet, and Tarin shook her head, as much to convince herself as him.

'I'm—I'm not coming down,' she said in a small, husky voice. 'It—there's nothing we have to say, and——'

'There's plenty I've got to say,' he argued, 'and you're going to listen!'

Tarin licked her lips in agitation. If only he'd given her some warning that he was coming, or if her uncle had—— She bit her lip, realising suddenly why Robert had taken the unusual step of going out for the evening and leaving her on her own. It seemed there was no need for any further co-operation between the McCourts and the Bruces—Robert and Darrel had already well and truly buried the hatchet and combined to leave her at Darrel's mercy.

'Are you coming down?' The brown eyes issued a challenge that was hard to resist, and she shook her head again, but with much less conviction, her pulses racing suddenly as she put two and two together.

'You—you organised this—you and Robert,' she accused, and his craggy, brown face split into a wide grin as he looked up at her.

'I told him I gave you until nine o'clock,' he informed her. 'It's now ten minutes past—time's up!' He narrowed his eyes for a moment and quizzed her. 'Which is it to be?' he asked softly. 'Do you come willingly or do I have to repeat Duncan's feat and break in?'

'You—you wouldn't dare!'

That, she realised almost immediately, was a mistake. The brown eyes glowed darkly at the challenge and he nodded his rough head. 'O.K.,' he said quietly. 'Have it your way!'

'Darrel!'

She leaned as far out of the window as was safe, but he had already disappeared again into the tiny porch over the front door and a second later she heard the rattle of the latch. Robert, of course, would have left it unlocked, and for a moment she felt as if her uncle had betrayed her.

Heavy footsteps on the stairs sent her hastily to the bedroom door and she opened it just as Darrel reached the half way stage on the stairs, looking out at him with her lips parted and a bright, glistening look in her eyes. He paused for a moment, looking at her, his own brown eyes warm and glowing and sending a shiver of anticipation down her spine.

'Well?' he queried softly, and raised a brow.

Tarin shook her head more by instinct than inclination, and she saw the swift gleam of white teeth in that craggy brown face as he started upwards again. 'Darrel!' Her cry had a light, husky sound and it did nothing to deter him. She ran from the room and on to the narrow landing, arriving at the top of the stairs just as he arrived there.

Without a word he put one arm behind her knees and lifted her, squirming wildly, up over his shoulder. She beat with her fists at the broad, unflinching back and tried to kick her legs, but she was too firmly held and he turned easily on the landing and started down again.

'Darrel! You—you savage! You—you bar-

barian!'

'Keep still,' he told her quietly, 'or I'll drop you!'

He took her through the tiny hall and as far as the front door before he put her down and Tarin thanked heaven that they had no near neighbours to witness the scene. She was breathing heavily and her eyes were bright and sparklingly blue as she looked up at him, straightening her dress with trembling hands and trying not to laugh, the way her instincts wanted her to.

He stood for a moment with his hands on his hips again, looking down at her with those bright, glowing brown eyes that sent shivers of anticipation along her spine like showers of ice water. Then he reached out with one hand and brushed the dark hair from her forehead, his long fingers gentle and almost sensual against the softness of her skin.

'History repeats itself,' he said softly, and she smiled without realising she was doing it.

'Not quite,' she argued. 'This time you had co-operation!'

'You're sure Duncan didn't?' he asked softly, and she shook her head, not at all sure. 'You said yourself,' he reminded her, 'that you thought she was in love with him.'

'I—I think she might have been.' She felt the thudding beat of her heart at her ribs and the fingers of both hands curled slowly into her palms as she looked at him. There was something about him, something that stirred such intense excitement in her that she could scarcely draw breath.

He was smiling and he reached out again, the long fingers curling about her neck and drawing her close, his other hand spanning her slender waist and adding its persuasion to that irresistible force. Warm, masculine scents enveloped her and she put her hands to the broad smoothness of his chest.

'Did you really think I'd let you leave me?' he asked softly, and his fingers tightened on her waist. 'Did you, Tarin?'

She sought for words, hardly daring to believe it was happening, and shook her head dazedly. 'I—I thought you—despised me,' she said breathlessly. 'I thought you hated me for being such a—such a——'

'Gullible little idiot?' he suggested softly, and laughed at her indignant face. 'Don't be so prickly, my darling, I didn't come here to fight with you!'

Tarin looked up at him, her blue eyes searching that craggy brown face, wondering if she would ever grow tired of simply looking at him. 'Why did you come, Darrel?' she asked softly, and he shook his head, a faint, ironic smile touching that wide mouth into mobility.

'Don't you know?' he teased gently. 'I have Deepwater back now, I'm independent, solvent and reasonably happy—but I need a wife!'

'You——' Tarin stared at him for a moment, hardly daring to believe she had heard him aright. 'Is—is that all?' she gasped. 'You—you want a wife and you think——' She tried to push him away with both hands, thrusting against the implacable strength of his arms. 'If that's all you came for,' she gasped furiously, 'you can go back and—and marry Gloria Stein! You *are* as bad as Duncan! That— that savage simply needed a wife too, and I suppose you think my pedigree guarantees I'll make a good one!'

'It proved a good match,' he said, unperturbed, and she did not notice the bright gleam of laughter in his eyes that teased her for her touchiness. 'After all, Jeanie gave him four good sons—what more could a man want?'

'You——' The rest of her protest was cut abruptly short when his mouth swept downwards swiftly and covered hers, his arms pressing her close to the virile hardness of his body until she had no breath left to object, even had she wanted to.

He felt warm and vibrant and excitingly ruthless, his hands both strong and gentle through the thin material of her dress, and she yielded to the urgent pressure he exerted, moulding her softness to him, drawing her resistance from her. His mouth was at once firm and persuasive, light and gentle on the smoothness of her throat and neck, the softness of her shoulders.

'Darrel!' She clung to him, afraid that she would wake at any moment and find this was no more than another hopeless dream, but it was real enough—that craggy dark face with its crown of reddish hair, and the brown eyes, glowing with an inner excitement she was only too willing to share.

She put up her hands and curled her fingers in the thickness of his hair, her bare arms warmed by the strong, smooth brown neck, her lips parted as she gazed up at him. He was more serious suddenly, one hand smoothing back the hair from her forehead again, the sensual touch of his long fingers shivering through her whole body.

'Don't you know yet that I love you?' he asked softly. 'I don't know whether you love me or hate me, but I do know that I mean to marry you, my prickly little McCourt, so don't try and fight me.'

'I won't!' She saw one brow lift in surprise, and laughed softly, shaking her head. 'Don't you know I've loved you for most of my life?' she asked him softly. 'I simply never grew out of loving you.'

He kissed her again so efficiently that she could only gaze at him with wide, blue eyes when he released her at last. 'And you'll marry me?' he asked.

Tarin nodded. 'Willingly,' she agreed breathlessly, and Darrel laughed.

'Well, that'll make a change!' he told her, and his mouth sought hers again, fiercely but curiously gentle. 'That hatchet is well and truly buried,' he said a few moments later, and sounded more than satisfied with the result.

romance is beautiful!

and Harlequin Reader Service
is your passport to the
Heart of Harlequin

Harlequin is the world's leading publisher of romantic
fiction novels. If you enjoy the mystery and adventure of
romance, then you will want to keep up to date on all of
our new monthly releases—eight brand new Romances
and four Harlequin Presents.

If you are interested in catching up on exciting and
valuable back issues, Harlequin Reader Service offers a
wide choice of best-selling novels reissued for your
reading enjoyment.

If you want a truly jumbo read and a money-saving value,
the Harlequin Omnibus offers three intriguing novels
under one cover by one of your favorite authors.

To find out more about Harlequin, the following
information will be your passport to the Heart of
Harlequin.